Praise for *I'm Not*

I'm Not Mad...I'm Special is a psy
the world through the teenager Sky Shanti's eyes, a young girl who's been deemed schizophrenic. She sees things that no one else sees. Believes things that no one else believes. Sky is a deeply troubled soul whose dalliances in black magic, drugs, and the need for revenge makes for the perfect breeding ground for something truly dark and sinister: something that our young Sky quickly learns to control and use for her own benefit of revenge against those who have wronged her. This one isn't for the faint of heart. There were a few times that I was glancing over my shoulder as I read. But if you are a lover of a good old-fashioned scary tales then *I'm Not Mad...I'm Special* is for you. Veronica Lamont has crafted a chilling tale that you won't be able to put down. You'll keep turning, page after stunning page, in an effort to figure this one out. But you'll be totally surprised by the twists that the author throws at you. The end will simply floor you because you'll never see it coming.

Reviewed by Sandra De Taranto, author of *Crying in the Rain*

* * *

Veronica Lamont has truly captured the psyche of Sky, the abused and vengeful main character, in this haunting book of the mind. Terrible things happen to those that have mistreated her, and Sky wants to be guilty. But how can she be guilty? She's locked away in a white-on-white padded room with nothing but her dreams to console her. Previously neglected, shunned, physically tormented, and falsely loved, Sky appeals to all readers who want to get even, and those readers will root for Sky and support her, they will wish that they could do what she does, and they, too, will want her to be guilty—guilty of delivering a deserved punishment.

The occult, the crimes, the vivid locales, and the cerebral insertions, all blend to make this book come alive with sympathy and empathy for Sky. Effortlessly flowing from one point of view to another, the story even propels the narrator into justifying the events. *I'm Not Mad...I'm Special* will make the reader dream and want to dream even more, dreamland being the place where all things are possible, especially justice, and the reader will be thankful for those dreams and then wake up and say YES to Veronica Lamont.

This reviewer received a pre-production copy of the text, and as with all such copies of books, there are wavers from proper presentation. Even so, the body of the story is powerful in its own right, and thorough editing can polish this gem to its rightful, unique shine.

Reviewed by Danny Lee Ingram, author of *Pennies on the Tracks*

* * *

In her first book, *I'm Not Mad...I'm Special*, Veronica Lamont tells the story of Sky Shanti, a schizophrenic teenager who faces the torment and torture of fellow classmate, Tina Robson. The story begins with Sky enduring yet another torturous day of Tina's relentless pranks, which pushes Sky over the edge. Institutionalized for psychological observation, Sky does her best to convince the staff and local law enforcement agents that she's responsible for a string of murders. Of course everyone just thinks she's crazy, but is she really?

Then she meets Lucy Jenkins, a young, single mother doctor at the mental hospital. Sky opens up to Lucy and tells her things she's never told anyone, like she can make her dreams reality. Lucy does her best to dig beneath the surface to discover the truth buried deep within Sky's mind. Veronica Lamont has written a truly spellbinding thriller. Though the dialogue may be disturbing or confusing at times, *I'm Not Mad...I'm Special* is a must read, filled with madness, black magic and a good old-fashioned dose of murder. Ms. Lamont has indeed proven with this first novel that she can weave a story of thrilling proportions. I'd keep a look out for future novels by this very talented first-time author.

Nicole Getridge, author of *Shielded Heart*

Sky is schizophrenic or that's what everyone else believes. As this story, reminiscent of *One Flew Over the Cuckoo's Nest* opens, Sky Shanti is enduring yet another hellish day at school. The usual butt of jokes, Sky has reached her limit when it comes to dealing with her nemesis, Tina Robson, after the most recent incident at school pushes Sky over the edge.

What happens next is pure psychological torture for not only Tina, but all those who have made Sky's life miserable in the past few months. Placed in an institution for psychological observation, Sky tries to convince the police and many of the staff at the mental facility that she is behind the murders of several people, though they don't believe her. Until she meets with a young doctor by the name of Lucy Jenkins. It is the manner in which Sky intends to prove herself to Lucy that propels the plot forward in this page turner filled with murder, madness and black magic.

First-time author Veronica Lamont has written an exciting psychological thriller, and must be commended for such a fine attempt for a first novel. While Ms. Lamont's lack of proper syntax and correct grammatical usage may confuse the reader at times, she more than makes up for it in her unique characters and compelling plot line. This is an author who has shown she can tell a story, and with experience and a little polish, she will provide many entertaining novels in the future. This reader/reviewer suggests you keep your eyes open for more of her tales, as they are wickedly delightful and will definitely provide some exciting reading ahead.

Reviewed by Denise M. Clark for Denise's Pieces,
author *Site & Book Reviews*

I'm Not Mad...
I'm Special

By
Veronica Lamont

PublishAmerica
Baltimore

First printing

ISBN: 1-4137-1425-0
PUBLISHED BY PUBLISHAMERICA, LLLP
www.publishamerica.com
Baltimore

Printed in the United States of America

Acknowledgments

Love and thanks to my family and friends who gave me their support when I needed it: Steve, Billie, Imogen and our dog, my dad, brothers and sister. Denise, Jerry, and their family. My best mate, Kelly, for spending many hours reading all my written works in its raw process and for being a great friend. Thanks to Michelle, Sue, and not forgetting little Mel, Vicky for her encouragement and her family, from America, I enjoyed spending time with them. And to everyone else I have not mentioned. Thanks also to PublishAmerica and their friendly support.

In loving memory of my mother
whom I miss dearly

Mother's Poem

Darkness fills the room
All is cold, there u lie. I dare not hold
Pale skin, white as white. I look long and hard
And I know you have reached the bright light

Sunshine with no fears, love with white sands
Crystal clear visions, a tender voice. A place to rejoice
I say goodbye…can you hear my voice
Such sadness do you know, this I will always show

Knowing this is as close to you as it will ever be
The feeling, the wishing, please don't let this be
Wanting, needing you to come back
Wondering why it was you and not me

Your brown hair swept to one side, your blue eyes shut
And your smile, smiles so silently
The room so small, but the love so big
It hurts; I still have more to give

I stand; I take your hand, so stiff
But I will leave knowing, you were a precious gift
You who gave me life, I will never forget
The things you gave and taught me

You opened my eyes and let me see,
Do not live this life in misery
I will teach my own the same thing, how to live and let be
You're never to be forgotten, you will always be near

~Poem written for my mother

WHO'S THE ODDBALL?

'Some people really do not have a clue. I am unique, and therefore, nothing like you. Only seventeen and I am already sick to the bottom of my stomach of infested humans that believe deep down inside that they are so much better than you or me. Somehow I just cannot seem to allow myself to indulge in such falsity as it floats around me.

'It is when I dream that I am able to be free, away from all of the deceit. I am in control of everything I want to be in control of, in my dreams where I hide away. What is more, that is everything that none of you could ever see or handle.

'Throughout my life already, I have met such false people, and at my humble abode was a life a child should never have seen. They would pick on me as if I was at fault. I was a pincushion, allowing them to stick their sharp pins into me. With each single prick that I received, it would make the hate settle deeper down inside of me, while the hot lava travelled around my veins, I could feel the pain waiting to explode. Now, I am able to laugh. In fact I can have the last laugh about Tina Robson. She was my worst nightmare. Many a times that misfit beat me. Even though to her, I was the oddball.

'I remember pulling the chain behind me, the piss water spinning in a corkscrew direction. As I left the toilet, after I zipped myself back up, to the right side of me I saw Tina with her two other mates, they were doing the same old practice in the mirror. I gave her some credit if any that she was, and I repeat was, very pretty. Even so, that is not what concerned me. No, it was the way she would make me feel, like the shit at the bottom of someone's shoe. As if stepping onto my face, into the stinking dirt left by lazy dog walkers who couldn't be bothered to clean up behind them. Tina as well as others made me feel like an unloved, beaten dog. However, that day was the final straw for me, the final day I would allow Tina to shadow me. Tina topped it off with her antics towards me that day, and helped with among others to change me into who I am now.

'I can still picture dashing quickly to the sink to wash my hands, and don't you just hate them bloody taps that run for five seconds and then you have to hit them again? I walked over to the hand dryer and pushed the big silver button, it felt like slow motion, from my visions around me. The noise twirled about the air, the voices that I could hear coming from over their direction were slurred, I could not make them out. I knew it was at my expense, their hullabaloo slowly drifted into my ear lobes. They were planning something. Then, I shifted fearfully over their way, hoping I would pass without having to pay for their cruelty, but with no such luck. Tina jumped out in front of me and pushed me back with her force. With the huge hold she had over me, I could only but just look and stare at her. Her skinny, long-legged body, long brown streaked hair, tanned face with a pair of big blue eyes, which glared evilly towards me.

'"*Well, well, if it isn't miss-pick-on-me-please. You're feeling brave. Do not think about trying to pass me without even saying hello*". These were the haunting words she said to me, I can still hear them to this day.

'"*Hello, Tina*". I said, feeling like a wimp. I had never felt the need to want to hurt someone so bad. I wanted to hurt her, no…I wanted to kill her.

'"*Well, it's a bit late for that now, isn't it? You're looking kind of…mmm…I would say tramp is the word that sums you up. And your hair, girl, why don't you do something with your hair? Here, look, why don't you let me have the pleasure in helping you*"? Tina nastily squealed, as she winked over to her other mates with her famous high and mighty stare. She then looked back at me.

'She floated towards me. I looked at her. With her tight denim skirt on, long enough to be a belt it was, who did she think she was? She had on a brown coloured pair of mid-length boots with wrapped buckles, and a glittered black one-sleeved top. The bitch had style but she was flirtingly tasteless. As she floated I did not even move, there really was no point. She then stuck her first finger into her mouth and slowly stretched out a chewy, stringy piece of white gum, walking around me pulling at it. Tina then stuck her face into mine, making me jump.

'"*This will help*". She smiled at me, making me feel anxious and with that, I felt one hand grab the back of my head fast. My hair filling her fingers and her other hand coiled around the chewy stringy piece of white gum right on the top of my hairline and downward. She pulled twisting and turning it into many a strand. I gave her no pleasure by reacting; I just stood waiting for her to finish amusing herself but inside I wanted to cry. I wanted to hurt her so badly. Things began to enter my mind. I knew I could get life behind bars, even to face the death penalty. I wanted to kill her and I did not know if this was a good thing or not. How could someone make me feel this way and get away with it? I just wanted to disappear and die.

'After about ten minutes of teasing and pushing, they left, taking my dignity with them, leaving me there on my own with white gum in my hair with a ripped silky navy blue blouse, one of my favourites. I looked into the mirror and the white gum beamed off my jet-black hair like a lonely glowing lamppost light on an empty, pitch-black street. I felt electric waves filter my body working its way to my head. The banging was intense.

'I closed my eyes and the visions then were horrific.... Beating Tina with a baseball bat gave me such hidden satisfaction. I opened my eyes and a small teardrop, one single, lonely drop, slipped down my rosy cheek, my green eyes looking like glass balls. Did I have a label that said "beat me" on my forehead? Did it say, "take the dignity away and leave it with a piece of fucking white gum"? I then left to go off to class with it still in place, just like a first-class loser. That bitch Tina once again successfully tarnished me.

'The school bell finally rang. I can still feel the ringing in my ears to this day, and as everyone hurried out heading for home, I slowly followed after them, still with the white gum in my hair and a few pointing fingers of laughter would come my way. That day was one of my worst days, but I had reached a point that I could handle it because of one thing; the words "revenge is sweet" would bounce around my brain box. From a young age, I believed in revenge. Some day, somehow, I would get even and have the last laugh.

'I was nearly home and before me stood another figure I loathed. Doesn't it just make you laugh; when you don't want to bump into anyone, you bloody bump into everyone.

'"*You silly child, get off this pavement, do not even breathe the same air as me, child*". These were the words Mrs Turner shouted to me. I just continued to walk past the old battleaxe that lived in the flats across from me, sending her evil looks. I was not in the mood for her. After the gum attack earlier that day at school, I tell you I was not in the mood. I just wanted to get home.

'"*Did you hear me, child? Just a silly child, that's all you are, you and your druggy family should go back to hell*". With that, I just turned towards her, I walked slowly to the old battleaxe Mrs Turner and finally I was face to face with her and I remember saying something like—

'"*I am sick, so sick of fools like you. Why don't you just go and die somewhere, you lonely cow? I mean, come on, look at you, you're like a hundred years old but act like flirty thirty, you have no friends and you stink. You are repulsive to look at, and I bet the only pleasure you receive is by sticking your broom handle up yourself each and every bastard night*". The old battleaxe, Mrs Turner, was stunned, I was stunned. That was the first time ever that I had the courage to face her or in fact anyone. I leaned over to her closer, feeling brave, and opened my mouth up wide getting ready to shout at her, and I stayed that way for a few seconds but felt more like minutes. Mrs Turner slapped across my face hard and once again, I was stunned. With that, I slowly but deeply breathed inwards and the air sat at the top of my throat waiting to gush out a long scream. "*Arhhhhhh*".

'I screamed from the top of my voice a continuous scream, which blew into her face. Mrs Turner placed her hands over her ears and stepped back. I then stopped. As I walked off, I left the words flowing her way. "*I will get you*". Then I headed off to my so-called family home, my auntie's home.

'When I entered, I went straight to the staircase and sat on the top step and knowing I could cry secretly, I cried my heart out, I cried once again in silence. After I had finished, I realised they were just more wasted tears I had let out, and that there was just no point in crying over spilt milk any longer. No one could hear nor help, so why waste the meaningless tears of mine? Why not just get even? Revenge is sweet.

'I was all alone in my bedroom, trying to remove all the traces of white gum that Tina had left with me that day. It would not budge. I started to look about my bedroom for a pair of cutters, next thing I knew my hair had huge chunks missing from it. I hated the reflection that glared back at me. Why was I so different, why? No one cared I was alone, no one has ever cared. The only time I could be free was in my dreams and in them I was in real control and I loved it. I could dream of whomever I wanted and be whomever I pleased.

'Still, until that night, that was the first night I was able to make things real from my head. I dreamt of something so shocking, even I was shocked. Yet, little did I know at first that my evil left my head and then wandered around my enemies. What do they call it? Premonition dreams, I think.

'I was over the two T's attack, Mrs Turner and Tina that would be, by the time I had popped pills and got drunk on sherry. Nevertheless, that was the night, the dark night that changed me into who I am now, and trying to explain what happened to me that night is hard. Hard because I know no one would believe me. I remember something dark entered my soul, something not from this world. Like a second sense, a second mind. My mind mused over the matter.

'After I had the soul-changing experience in my dream, in my bedroom, but felt like reality, Miss Tina herself stood before me and then more came. The old battleaxe, Mrs Turner from the flats across the road from me, and then Jimmy the wanker that always threw stones at my head. All of a sudden, I had the people I hated with a passion standing there lined up inside my dark dream. But why, I did not understand. The meanings from my visions, I could not figure it out, until I realised after the first murder, what I had done after cutting the huge chunks out from my hair, then I knew what I had done. It then became clear. Finally something I had done had meaning, something I cannot yet explain to others.

'It was the weekend, the next morning after my sticky white gum attack, and school was a long way away from me and the bad haircut was the least of my worries. Last night I realised that I could do things that life itself did not create. I heard a deep whisper in my dreams by a creation I had developed from within but took place from without, that I could do whatever I liked. ANYTHING. Even so, I was still very confused.

'I looked into the mirror and suddenly I saw what I saw, vaguely from in my dark dream, from the dark night before, my hair was back to its normal length. The huge black chunks were gone that I had cut and the colour had changed to a blonde shade. Amazing, but confusing. I had to look twice, and I loved the new look. This free feeling, this free control, was astounding me, but I now felt something that I have never had the chance to feel before. I now felt whole. So, the next night I dreamt some more. I dreamt that Mrs Turner had a very unfortunate accident, but it was not until I awoke that following morning I watched the local news eating my breakfast, I nearly choked. Mrs Turner on the news, dead, battered. Shit, Mrs Tuner was dead.

'That is when I sat in total shock. I tried to unravel my befuddled mind and yes, premonition is the right word, while pure exhilaration roared within me'.

* * *

SKY sat in her first interview since arriving at the mental institution, on the charges of murder she could soon face, or be it the conclusions from professional doctors that sat opposite her; they faced a permanent in-patient at their overbearing establishment, which held already over a hundred sad cases.

Sky told her events repeatedly, while no one mentally took in her over-ridden stories with her dark cries for help, as they sat and listened. Only the blue fountain pen scrawling the paper that took on her embellished accounts she shared. She needed to face the padded cell…they believed.

TO BELIEVE OR NOT TO BELIEVE

As I lay on yet another boring April spring morning, I can see the long white coats rushing towards me, with their pricking tools. I shouted at them.

'Get off me, you're all insignificant fools, I wish you all pain. GET OFF ME NOW'! They were holding me down tight and pulling at the fasteners that held my white straight jacket, the only secure thing they had to stop me from attacking them.

'Calm down, Sky, now there really is no need to panic. Just settle down, please'.

A pair of brown eyes looked at me. He wore a white coat that I could see from his thin neck and down. A hospital nurse asked while tightly holding on to my left arm above my elbow as he smiled. His cheap aftershave scent skipped up my nose, smelt like two days worth of dried sweat. They think I'm mental. They were treating me as a mental patient, while keeping me in this condition with their questions. Give me a break I thought. They did not understand my powers and me, so what is the point in answering their questions? Their questions never made sense; I wish they would just stop repeating them...shut up please, making me feel nauseous while my head hammered inside. I shouted 'Blah blah fucking blah' at them. Them figures, with long white coats and them protection words, they were discussing the next hit to make me calm and sleepy, asking me about miss-pick-on-me-please Tina Robson. She is dead, who cares, no one's missing her. I know I'm not.

They had no idea. I have told them continually that I killed her. I killed them all. What is the problem here? I'm confused. They're the ones that should be wearing this white stiff jacket. I'm special and they just hate this fact. I am going to sue the whole bloody lot of them, stinking procedures and laws. You do not have the right to suffocate me any more. 'Just stick that needle in me', I kept pleading. 'Make me sleep. Take me home', I wished.

The prick holes seeped with hate that formed my battered soul, prick,

prick, and prick some more. My body went stiff after yet another sharp prick entered into my arm. I could no longer see those big brown eyes that looked down at me, I knew exactly what they were doing. They were dosing me up again. Let them get on with it if it pleased their huge egos then, let them carry on. They were trying to shut me up, trying to make me give out information they wanted to hear on the murders, twisting my words, making me look the fool. Besides, by retaliating they would prick me. Why does everyone fucking prick me? I'm Sky, the pincushion, come on, prick me.

When they shut that door after that sharp prick and the drugs would gradually make me sleep, they did not even realise they were doing me a favour. It was where I felt at home in my dreams as I drifted away from the cold bleak room. Far, far away from the figures in long white coats I would glide. The fools, no matter how hard they tried, could not take my powers from me. They rejected the truth and continued to ask more questions about my sanity. I kept hearing their crap repeatedly inside my pounding mind. You are mad! You are crazy! Did you kill them victims of yours? There is no proof whatsoever that they link with you. You need professional help. She is barmy, lock her up and throw away the key.

These words echo within me, words that travelled around my mind continuously…I often spoke to myself all day, every day. In fact, I asked the questions and then I answered them. The only voice that made any sense to me was my own.

As I drifted, which I had no control over as the drugs dragged me away from been cognisant, I saw the dead battleaxe, Mrs Turner, under my sleepy eyelids. The pleasure was all mine when I recollected the actions of my evil….

MRS TURNER SHORT AND SWEET

She's greying on the sides with a tilted pair of glasses falling onto her ageing nose, as she reads a love story, a Mills and Boons tacky tale. This was the lady who Sky hated immensely; the one she had lined up in her dark dreams with the other victims she wanted to kill. Which Sky did kill?

The old girl, Mrs Turner, made Sky's life hell, from a list of nastiness varying from verbal abuse to a broken run-over bike to the confrontation the pair had on the day of Sky's gum attack. Why Sky? Well, it was not just Sky she picked on, Mrs Turner really hated kids...she hated all kids.

Beside her on the dirty pine chest of drawers, next to the phone and pink tissues, the clock turned to 11.00 p.m. The electric fan was on, blowing in every corner, while making her tea go cold quicker than normal. Mrs Turner was lost too deeply into her story to even notice how late it had become, and forgetting she had even made herself a cuppa in her old chipped Garfield cup.

Not often blinking but her breathing short and husky, she flipped a page over. As she moved her head and eyes, drifting once again to the start of that new page, suddenly out of fan-blowing thin air her head jerked forward fast, knocking the book onto the bedcover. Her face left an outline print in between her legs on her floral designed old-fashioned duvet, as she pulled herself back up. Her nose was bleeding and trickling downwards to her lips, a feeling like a loose hair floating freely with an annoying tickling sensation. Her hand wiped over the red coloured liquid in panic, smudging the blood around her left cheek.

Jumping back in shock and gasping for air, her body was somehow pushed violently off the bed onto the dirty pink coloured carpet tiles. Her back arched as she curled up into a tight ball, trying desperately to stop the pain. Mrs Turner's face turned a pale shocked colour, minus the tilting glasses.

Her body was moving around, fast, not like a fit but more as if someone was kicking her in the abdominal area, her body moving to an unseen action as the blood dripped onto her yellow flowered nightdress.

Weeping whilst trying to crawl across the floor to the bed to pull herself back up, her eyes were now as red as rubies and blood flowed off her pale mature chin like the last few raindrops falling from a half-dead leaf. Wheezing and grabbing, her body flew once again across the room, sounds of old fragile bones cracking, before her.

Mrs Turner desperately sought help and explanations for the hows and the whys. No one was there and she was being beaten black and blue, her body physically smashed in as if she had arranged a boxing fight with an invisible Mike Tyson, with his foul play. Her leg bent the wrong way, like a flexible dolly, and her left arm felt floppy with no motion. Her right eye had swollen inwards and three teeth were visible as they flew out from her red-marked mouth, but still her body jerked about in her empty bloodstained bedroom. Mrs Turner's death was brief, and Sky was so pleased....

IT'S ALL ON THEIR PART

The room that was cold and bleak, as I came around from the drugs' effects, filled with light. Maybe the light symbolized passing from this hell to my new gates of heaven. The door opened and in walked yet again more figures with long white coats, my demons. Looking over me, I saw again a pair of big brown eyes. I felt rough tugging at my buckled jacket. They were unstrapping me from this hard table bed, the only place that felt like home to me. More questions, their questions, same answers, my answers, what do they expect from me I didn't know. I did not know much anymore. How long had I been here? I came here fine and now I'm feeling the strain and I really think they're trying to make me mad. It's all on their part, doing what others had done to me in my past. It is sick, I'm all good, I'm all normal. It is they, believe me...really, it is all of them.

* * *

Now sitting in a chair, in a room on my own, they had no respect, I tell you. I was waiting for something to happen. I looked around and saw only a white table with a lonely old tape recorder sitting on top. Two other white chairs and a matching white clock opposite me that made too much noise, a noise of haunted secluded boredom.

A big mirror behind me took up nearly the whole wall, and that too was an off-white colour. Was this a sick fashion statement or what? Everything that is mad or is associated with being mad is fucking white? However, I knew the mirror was double-sided, just like in the films. Of course it was, it was not there for me to check out my appearance. To tell the truth, I was confused about my appearance by now.

'So, Sky, why do you think you're here'? Half an hour later, going by the white mad clock on the wall but feeling much longer, I was imposed on by a women who looked like she had no clue. She was sitting in front of me like

Miss Lady Muck.

'I don't know, why am I here'?

'You're here because three weeks ago you were found at a murder site and ever since we have been studying you and your unsafe behaviour'.

I did not even know what day it was, never mind how many that had past. What a load of crap, three weeks. Had I really been here that long, already?

'So tell me, what did you and your clever cronies come up with?Not a lot, I assume, and don't bullshit me. My "unsafe behaviour", I'm as sound as a pound, fool, what are you chatting about, what do you mean? You don't even know me'.

Tapping my feet on the floor, I was tempted to take a quick look at myself in the mirror to see how I was shaping up.

'Well, to be blunt then, Sky, we do know you are in need of help, a lot of help. You have a double personality and you have a very high IQ level, which means you are intelligent and know what is going on around you. We have diagnosed that you have high levels of imagination, and your double personalities are one of good and bad. As for the doctor, when you first arrived here at the hospital, you bit his right cheek and kicked him in his lower body area. For your information he had to undergo an emergency operation'. Sky laughed. The Miss Lady Muck looked at her in disgust but carried on.

'So there was your bad side. Your good side was what we saw in your profile from school reports, teachers and friends' statements and this one personality you only have when it suits you, so we're told and have learned'.

She looked at me as if I was still a school kid. It had felt like a while now since being in school, but it had only been about nine weeks. I had left school the cold January weekend I had to cut my hair because of white stringy sticky gum that Tina had left with me.

'So'? I looked on, thinking how boring this bird was becoming. Her and a secluded boring white fucking mad clock, I was in a no-win situation. I feel the suffocation, I feel the desire to lash out, but I won't.

'What do you want from me? I have told your cronies again and again that I killed all of them; do you want me to tell you again? By the way, I do not have friends. Get your facts right'.

The Lady Muck sat back into her chair. She knew the account, but nope, they did not believe and now she does not believe, going by her facial expressions.

'So you're still sticking to the same story you have told us, Sky? Well, I will read it to you once more and then you tell me if you want to change anything', Lucy, the doctor, insisted. I said, 'Whatever'.

'On the 16th of March 2002, you were found at the family house of Miss Tina Robson. She was raped. She was strangled and beaten. Her body was smashed in more than one hundred places. We are still waiting for the forensic tests to come in, to tie up some loose ends, but we are certain all that blood in her room was her own. Now obviously you, yourself, did not on your own commit this sick act. That is if you had anything to do with it in the first place, as you have been telling us'. Lucy took a breather. 'You couldn't possibly have done all this to her. Now, you seem to persist it was all you, but there are no links that link you to her murder so far, only the one fact that you were present at the crime scene on your own, sitting on the fence when the police arrived'.

Pause, a long pause.

'Even to the other murdered victims, murdered at the start of March, March 2nd to be precise, for a Mrs Turner and March 9th for a Mr Jimmy Johnston, but still there are no links. So therefore, we would like to know why you are adamant about this. We believe you know who did this. We would think it's in your best interest to tell us, and we know you know something from the details you have told us. You could have only known by being there, hence being found at the scene'.

I was right. They had come up with nothing, and I love it when I am always right. The Miss Lady Muck could talk for England. I think she just liked the sound of her own voice. I definitely felt like she was mocking me, chatting to me as if I was a child still, looking down at me with authority.

Now firstly, I had never fully explained to them about my dreams or how I created them. Having taken full part in the crimes, as it was my head they were coming from in the first place, it was my magic and my weapon, and this I kept a secret. I just told them...well, I let them believe I had physically been there and done it all. I am playing mind games and I am winning.

Yet, fact is, I only really took part in this by being asleep on my bed in my room dreaming such madness that filled me with joy. Mrs Turner, now, she was easy. She was my first, she died while I slept and dreamt it. But after her I had left it for a week or so before I got to Jimmy, his too being easy, more of a test really just to make sure I wasn't imagining things, and I wasn't. Then I realised I could dream it first and then be there when it physically happened or I could dream it and whilst I dream it, it happens. How clever is that!

As time passed, I also realised that I could make things happen that no one could see but me. Like with my hair that somehow I made grow back and change colour, from the chunks I cut, trying to remove sticky white gum. Only I could see it, but it happened.

Mind you, though, no one commented on it the next day when I awoke, and that puzzled me, but it happened because I saw it. Really, I did see it. Then suddenly it did become clear to me that other people could not see what I could see, and what I was changing. It became clear that my powers were a secret. I told no one.

Secondly, the deaths were the only thing that reality could have the pleasure in seeing and trying to explain. I knew that was true, it was on the news for fuck's sake. At first, I did not understand why others could not see anything else but the deaths. My mind was going mad one minute and then the next I was on a magical high.

I was so high that night, I changed into who I am now. I hardly remembered any of the chanting ceremony that I performed; only that darkness entered my soul, something not from this world, like a second sense, a second mind. Mind over matter. I started to understand.

'What colour is my hair'? I asked in a testing manner as I broke the long silent pause.

'What does this have to do with anything I have just said to you'? the Lady Muck enquired raising her eyebrows in confusion.

'What is the colour'?

'Black, Sky, your hair is black'.

I stood and walked over towards the mad off-white coloured mirror. I felt her eyes watching my every move. I walked right up to it, and not to my surprise because I was not bloody mad in the first place, I knew the colour of my hair was blonde, still blonde from when I changed it. I knew it. They are just trying to make me mad, them people in long white coats, but I still knew it was blonde. I could for crying out loud see that it was bloody blonde before my own very eyes.

'You're full of shit, it's blonde. Can't you see it's blonde'? I shouted to her.

'Sky, your hair is black. Can't YOU see that'?

I turned and looked at her with an evil frown, from her sarcastic style, and then I looked back at my reflection, again I saw blonde.

'You're making me think it's black, it's not black. Are you blind or what? I know your game, you're trying to make me mad, it's all you. It's all you, you, you, you'! I shouted sticking up my middle finger to her. I really had a stomach full of her by now and the indigestion was hurting me deep down inside, I could feel the boiling acid erupt.

I started smashing my head against the mirror, again and again, looking right into the eyes that hid behind the glass, knowing they were there watching me.

Banging more, blood spitting everywhere, kicking and head butting, I continued.

'I know what you're doing, wey hey, hahaha, you can't break me. I see you and I can feel you, my hair is blonde, did you hear me in there? Did you hear me in there'? I screamed.

I pushed my face up close to the mirror and started to blow on it, my breath hitting the glass and being sucked back in as I gasped for more air. Making my mouth bigger and sticking my tongue in and out, my eyes were wide open, while blood dripped to the floor bouncing in half making smaller drops, red stuff everywhere.

In rushed four security guards and three doctors. Lucy stood by the small red alarm button by the wall, her hand still firmly pushing on it as she watched on in astonishment. Sky turned and saw them slowly walking towards her like a pack of wolves. She stepped back six spaces and started to do a strange jig in one spot on the floor. She pushed her mouth and lips outwards in a pouting shape, like trout lips, together with her eyebrows rising up and down, making faces in a rhythmic movement. Sky shouted 'blonde' continually.

Running head first into the double-sided mirror with all her might, she knocked herself flat out. She fell into her own blood pool. She lay knowing her hair was blonde. Her last screaming blood-spitted word was blonde, but to the others who stood in that room, they only saw the colour black.

THANK THE WORLD FOR WALKING BUTTERFLIES

This soul-changing experience Sky encountered in her dream, was it just merely a dream? No, it was not. Something did change her, something so strong but inexplicable. From a young age, Sky suffered at the hands of her parents. They were strong drug addicts with vivid imaginations. Her mother did not hesitate, not once while pregnant, to drop pills and lick her many partners' king-size papers, to seal the cannabis all the way until her labour day and thereafter.

Neglected Sky suffered years of misery and lack of confidence. No one noticed she was ever there. From the young age of seven, she had the knowledge of a higher level, with her own drug binge in her wardrobe and her invented visual affects that kept her safe within her so-called real world.

Her interest of the other side kept Sky busy after school hours. Being high, she would read up and play on ouija boards and cast witches' spells. It was mostly in her head that she was potent and she believed that this way of life was her only friend.

When closing her eyes and entering into a world of colours and flowing love, with big blue apple trees and walking butterflies with flying cats, her world was the safer world until she devolved hate. Then her peace dreaming became more destructive. That night she did have a soul-changing experience. Something dark did enter her soul, something not from this world; she felt a second sense, a second mind. She had the power to change everything she wanted in her dreams. To world peace to World War Six, even to female cartoon characters with builders' bums on the building sites whistling at passing males. That night did happen. What happened was under the influence of drink and drugs with a hint of dream spells that she had conjured up. Her own masterpiece taken from all different spells she had learnt from over the years. To her, the stringy sticky white gum played an important roll in her efforts to perform and succeed in her dreams that night.

Being Sky was not at all easy, growing up around mindless groupies that spent their hours throwing blast parties and taking drug cocktails that could blow you away.

A grubby three-bedroom council house was shared by two different people, not including Sky and her mother, with her selection of "pick a mix" blokes while her father was in la la land. The mix constituents of LSD, a forceful hallucinogenic drug that bit you with a painstaking psychoactive upshot, extreme obsession and high visions, with a twist of other drug cocktails and a hit of Big C, was coming from the corner of the living room, their hideout. The "pushers lounge".

Being Sky and living around the "pushers lounge", she learned nearly every drug by name and nick. She learned what to mix and what not to mix. She even learned the size packages being prepared and measurements for the sales on the streets. It was easy moneymaking. What a trouble-free life it was for any amateur or professional of the world doing this. Even if you got yourself something small, you still could make monies.

Like a bar of hash for £250 (that's if you had a friend as a dealer or you would be looking at £380 range). That bar weighed 238 grams, and from that one bar you would get eight and half ounces at 28 grams per ounce and the half being 14 grams. Selling these drugs in 8ths, getting eight 8ths from one ounce at penny measurements, for £10 each, you ended up with plenty to sell. Then you would make £430 profit after paying the dealer the £250. Something so painless and simple could all be sold in one day, like hot cakes, do it every day and then you're laughing. I guess you would say it was easy money; no wonder the young people chose this route first. Sky even sold to some guy that called around one evening and she was home alone. Sky encountered many dealings at an age of eight onward...JP's memory of dealing stuck out the most....

* * *

A young Sky laughed to herself at the weird character that stood before her.

'Oi, girl, got any speed ere in ya gaff'?

'Yes, plenty here, come in'. She pulled the door open. She knew JP (Jean Paul) and found him highly amusing, very ugly, skinny and wriggly, but she never judged him as all the others did. That is why she could relate to him, as he was the one the groupies picked on the most.

She was so young and watched a grown up once too often risk their life for a hit of anything they could get their hands, mouth and nose on. But Sky secretly was in their league, in some cases maybe even in a higher league.

She watched him shuffle over to the single black burnt hole-looking chair, as if waiting for a waitress to bring a menu of killers to him. Sky headed out of the lounge and five minutes later came back and lobed a clear plastic bag over to JP. He didn't see it coming and it slapped him smack on the forehead.

'Sorry', she giggled. He just grinned at her with his yellow teeth.

'That's free, JP, but don't tell no one, if they say anything I just act dumb. They're way too high to even notice me, never mind missing drugs'.

He looked at her with a sad expression but then winked and jumped up to the table. Sky watched his excitement. He started to chop at his free white powder with a blade that already existed on the table, next to a burnt tin with at least an eight fag mix in it and a red coloured bong that bent this way and that way, empty beer cans with half-smoked joints in overfilled ashtrays.

'Enjoy', she said. She heard the hard snorting taking place while leaving the room.

'Nice one girl, nice one'. He raised his arm up in gratitude, not knowing she was gone already. The rest of that evening she spent upstairs alone in her room, locked away from the outside, never being too careful of them randy blokes that came in and out all night long, high as a kite feeling horny. Sky had already experienced their vile attitudes....

* * *

I awoke, looking up at the ceiling of the cold bleak room I now called home. Feeling faint and coming around from numbness, from my head breakdancing with a double-sided mirror. Feeling quite mellow considering my facial area was hurting, feeling as if I had no control over anything that could move on my face, I tried to look over to the side of me. I knew someone's presence was among mine, but the cuts would not allow me to see as far as I needed to.

'What do you want'? I slowly demanded. I waited for a reply, but nothing. I closed my eyes slightly and saw dots. Small black dots growing slowly into squares then into triangles and slowly introducing different luminous colours making astonishing swirls. They started to form into a figure, like a faded clown with red tears wearing a baby gown. Slowly but surely the figure became clear, the figure I tried so hard to please and receive some recognition from. 'Dad'.

Then within that figure pushed out yet another slowly forming to shape once again. Like a devil with green wings, with my double-edged dagger sticking out from her heart area. That, too, slowly changed to a figure that played no particular role in my life. 'Mum'.

Sky said these names aloud. Lucy stood from the chair as she heard Sky mutter and saw her coming back around.

'Hi, Sky, it's Miss Jenkins, we have met already. I have been assigned here to do further tests and questioning, but I thought it would be better for you to meet me in your room, after your mirror performance. It would be safer. I hope you do not mind'.

Miss Jenkins was trying to be nice, trying to get on the right foot this time with Sky after the earlier recital and the meeting not going so well. Lucy wanted to show her caring side, thinking maybe it would help them two to bond more than the other doctors that had tried already, but they just treated her like an object or a testing piece to help calculate their findings.

'Mum, I wish I was at home with you, I don't like it here, I miss everyone'. Sky had a one-way conversation with her parents.

'Yes, I know, I know, I'm feeling as if no one is paying me any attention'.

Miss Lucy Jenkins stood and watched the closed-eyed Sky communicate to thin air, taking mental notes on her actions, entranced by her sad face.

'Okay, if you say so, Dad. I know, yes, I will win the game, I will keep it up'.

Sky slowly slipped back into her la la land, to a place very similar to where her daddy used to go, drifting to a far place that had no recall of life in the mental hospital. Sky's mind would drift all the time, her mind a messed-up place.

Nevertheless, did that mean she was mental or mixed up? Did that mean her actions were self-inflicted or merely the cause of child neglect, or a dirty disease roaming her mind that showed itself to the world? Who knows the identification of her ways? Was she schizophrenic, psychotic or insane? Are they one and the same or is one worse than the other? Are we all too late to help her, will she die a sad case and will we never understand her? Society is so far behind on facts, does she deserve to be an outcast? What exactly is a mental patient? Who was responsible for this girl's anger: was it you, society, or me?

Who exactly is going to face punishment for this crime placed upon a person shown nothing but distasteful behaviour?

The fact is this. Schizophrenia is a disease. It is ill health of one's brain. There is no race, sexual category, or preference; the disease likes to strike its favourite age group, sixteen to twenty-five, worldwide. However, in total, it can affect anyone or everyone, any age, any time and for any reason.

Deforming of the senses, physical and biochemical changes in the brain giving solid indication of changed personality, a different dimension to reality, hallucination, and incapability to care for themselves or others.

So therefore, this is not self-inflicted or born and spread from past accounts or parental neglect or bullying. This will attack you if you want it or not and, as there are many treatments available, there is no cure. The symptoms can be brought under control in days, weeks, months, even years depending on the person and the degree to which he or she may suffer the infestation. Sometimes, you will get worse before you get better; the side effects are one downfall to any treatment given.

Some side effects are sickness, loss of appetite, constipation, and dry mouth, becoming excited or fretful. Then you are fed more medication to help with the side effects. Procyclidine will help with the uncontrollable shaking, the annoying twitches, the long restless flights, and the weird body movements.

However, what is worse for Sky and her fellow hospital patients, her newfound friends? Is it the side effects, or the enduring group meetings, or the industrial physical work groups? Maybe the daily smells of disinfectant from the high rule of both personal and living hygiene. Alternatively, it could be the sharing of wards full of thirty-plus violent, shy, greedy, lying, foaming-from-the-mouth companions. The early nights and early mornings of boredom and self-hate, the very routine that takes your every breath.

Or could it be the loneliness, being trapped by your own bubble in your own blown up world, and you can't get out or bring anyone into it, and no one wanting to share it with you. Treating you like an infested dumb dead head. The not knowing of when or where, if ever, you will share a tender moment with a loved one again.

As the urge you once had has now truly become a lost stain, like the white stains on one's bed, just washed away on a hot washing circle, the urge placed under control by a medication you now needed to stop your malfunction. In fact…who gives a fuck?

SKY SHANTI: THE ORANGE FOLDER CONCEALED A LOT

Sky Shanti was born January 1985, no complications at birth. Mother a Sally Shanti and father Jacob Shanti, no siblings. Leaving home address: 106 Hipslip Chestnut Walk, London. In 1994, her parents were killed in a drug battle, shot dead in the family home.

Sky witnessed the whole event. This was the first time Sky came to our attention. At the time, Sky was given early care for shock. Sky moved to her auntie's house still in the same London area: 12 Redsleet Dove Close, London. No court order placed, only continuous care was given and medical help.

Lucy flipped from start to finish of the orange folder in no particular order, digesting the information as she sat back down, once again waiting for Sky to come around from the drug's effect. She had seen many cases in her six years in the mental institutions and she did not see this to be much of a difference from any other patient's case she had read. All cases vary but are of a similar nature: alcohol, and drugs, depression related with twists from their lives they were shown…or not shown, in some cases.

Lucy did feel sorry for Sky's life and that she had no, or been shown to have any likelihood for success. This life was full of mentally ill no-hopers, but nine times out of ten, it results back to their early childhood, an event, or abuse and lack of help from their guardians. It festers away, eating their entire existence, forming them into a hard nutshell. And in that hard nutshell sits quietly and waits, a rotten nut…so to speak.

Lucy continued to read the words that summed up a single human being's outlook on life they faced.

Sky was in a negative home among the higher level of neglect. Drugs were the basis of the family home and the daily activities of selling and taking of all first-class drugs. Sky had shown all levels of antisocial behaviour with no continuous adult care given. Our lack of involvement meant we did not know of any abuse until after her parents' deaths.

Sky's records of schooling shows very frequent attendance, most likely due to the only place she could seek solace. As to her admitting to being a drug user herself, tests were given over a period.

It was apparent that the conclusions found were of high delusional patterns of an unfunctional child. Sky is sanctioned to take the following medication: mild doses of Depixol.

Recognising physical and behavioural symptoms, and her decrease to attention, her isolation being a big issue, according to her auntie. In addition, at times becoming very negligent to her, being irritable, angry and constant mood swings. She was diagnosed with a mild form of schizophrenia at that time. Also, at the time of this testing, her auntie took on a full role in her recovery alongside professional help.

Lucy started to itch her red coloured hair with the pen she was slightly tapping. Black bags sat under her tight-framed brown eyes. Her mouth wide open from yawning, she displayed perfect white teeth. Catching up on paperwork was difficult, and her seven-year-old did not help any, trying to convince Mummy to let her share the comfortable double bed her mother used. Lucy then tried to convince her daughter that sleeping in her own bed was the right thing to do, but really, it was for peace and quiet. She suggested in the end by promising to take her to the cinema the following night to watch *Cats and Dogs*. Bribery…a helpful tool, all mothers have it. She carried on with the orange folder, but in the back of her mind, she was wondering how Cindy's day at school went.

Professional help was only given to Sky for a limited period of time due to her aunt moving and not forwarding a follow-up address, so therefore this help came to an inclusive stop.

> Furthermore, tests taken since 25th March 2002, having been found at the murder site of one Miss Tina Robson murdered on the 23rd March 2002, it has become clear that her diagnosis is much worse than previously predicted. Sky from the start has been claiming it was solely herself who committed these crimes. And brought to our attention from herself that she also murdered a one Mrs Turner, along with a Mr Jimmy Johnston. Now these claims have been dismissed due to no links being found via the police investigation. The case is still undergoing more inquiries as Sky still continues to claim involvement. Police and doctors concerning Sky Shanti will be in close contact for further results. Sky is on suicide watch for her own safety and others. This will continue until further notice.

Lucy had by now refocused and realised the time and that she had dazed most of it sitting in that room waiting for Sky to awake while picturing Sky's images as a child. She decided to collect her belongings together and leave it until the following day and then she quietly left to entertain her daughter with popcorn and the film *Cats and Dogs*, as she had promised the small child.

* * *

Moments after the door shut, Sky's green eyes wildly opened as if enchanted by something dark with a wicked smile across her cut face. She started singing to herself in a high screaming pitched voice.

'Here weee...go round the mulberry bush the mulberry bush the mulberry bush here weeee...go round the mulberry bush on a cold and frosty morning'.

* * *

Lucy arrived home in plenty of time to cook before heading to the movies. She pulled up to her two-bedroom house. It was quite small but big enough for the two of them, her child and herself. She had kicked out her daughter's cheating father a year ago after catching him cheating on her marble kitchen floor with the babysitter. She allowed him only fortnightly visits on one condition: that he was constructive with her and stuck to the rule of their child not meeting his young mistress at any point whatsoever. He did stick to that. He loved his child, unlike Sky's parents.

Lucy could never fully comprehend why people had children that they could not care for. Lucy took every care of Cindy's needs; she only worked three days on, three days off so she could be there as much as she could for her. She had Mrs Smith take care of Cindy when she worked. Mrs Smith was like a real nanny to her, not just a job title. She cared, and she loved spending her time with little Cindy.

Lucy's night turned out to be an expensive but fun evening. After the movies Cindy begged her mum to take her bowling, and of course, Lucy gave in. Lucy was much of a loner; her world was her child and her work. Lucy lacked the skills to interact with another male but she secretly was lonely and in need of some tender loving care. She was content with life around her, and knowing she would not be alone forever, she felt she did not need to look for the opposite sex in any manner. It was not because she could not pull a bloke. She had striking dyed red hair in loose curls that bounced around freely, small tight-framed brown eyes, and a silky complexion. She certainly had a good-looking style about herself, so she could have any bloke she wanted, if she had the time.

* * *

Sky was coming back around from sleep to reality in her cold bleak room a mile away from where Lucy lived. Her one-sided scary conversations and strange singing had stopped. She was shaking her head from side to side and still in a straight jacket for fear of self-harm. Sky's case proved to be on high alert. Underneath this hard and non-caring Sky was a deeply depressed, sad Sky. The wanting to cry, the wanting to be with someone she could relate to and at this point even JP (Jean Paul) would have done. Never knowing or hearing the words 'I love you, Sky' or the hugs that children got before bedtime. Only a joint or a wrap of speed would comfort her while Mummy and Daddy played their roles to the wrong people. Even when her parents were shot, Sky was hidden under the kitchen table with the last words from her mother shouting, '*Jacob, quick! Chuck the fucking coke down the toilet! It's the police*'! It was not the police, it was a drug war, East against South, and they lost. After they had left with the house trashed, and three dead bodies, Kim being the third, an 18-year-old who had no direction in life but that 'pushers lounge'. Sky had to alert the police and she just sat alone in the corner of her purple-walled bedroom until they had arrived. Sky was not even sobbing from her visions, the police observed as they walked in, and it was noticeable that the young girl was in deep shock. They shifted her to a safer place. Her auntie's soon followed.

Sky never fully took on board the loss of her parents; she never spoke one word of the incident or even grieved, but she now in thin air has conversations with them. Perhaps she never realised they had even passed.

PROOF DON'T MEAN THAT YOU'RE ANY CLOSER TO CONCLUSION

Lucy arrived at work the following sun-kissed day at around 8.30 a.m. with a hot cup of sugarless tea from the vending machine before entering the lift to the 16th floor. The doors automatically opened with a voice tone like a robot saying 'Doors opening…16th floor'. She stepped out, heading to the office for part-time use only, up a long disinfected grey-stoned corridor. She opened the door and walked in, closing it behind her. Sitting at her large light oak desk, she threw off her pinstriped jacket, size eight, to one side and opened her leather briefcase taking out her overdue work and once again Sky's case folder. 'Come in'! Lucy shouted from the knocking of the door, and in walked the receptionist for that floor, her name was Sara.

'These were faxed in this morning for you, Miss Jenkins. Also, here are the reports you wanted'. The receptionist handed the faxes and the reports then smiled and left. 'Thanks'. Lucy's words chased the receptionist before she shut the door behind herself. The receptionist was your young 'typical blonde' nail-filing type, only good for one thing…keeping quiet.

Lucy browsed the faxes with her anticipation flowing from her. In her hands were the DNA and fingerprints results to Mrs Turner, the first murder case, and a fully completed outline on the murder, scene and conclusions. Reading on, her facial expressions were of an alarmed look, a shocked look, and her brown, small, tight-framed eyes lit up. 'Well, I never' is what she said aloud. Lucy, still knew in the back of her bamboozled mind, knew that they had to wait for the other two victims cases to come in, meaning she felt that they were a long way away from solving this case. DNA and fingerprinting and further tests took time and patience. Lucy's patience was wearing thin as she headed out from her office to face her meeting with Sky.

'Good morning, Sky', Lucy said as she sat opposite her. Again, in that same room, Sky turned nutty. The mirror had been replaced and showed no existing account of her explosive behaviour from the other day.

'Whatever', a moody Sky muttered back. Lucy started to flick through her folder and then looked towards Sky in a searching way.

'Sky, I have some new information on the murders that I want to run with you. We now have DNA and fingerprint results concerning Mrs Turner'.

'Ooh, poor her', Sky joked and smirked, the tip of her tongue licking the side of her mouth. Lucy continued.

'It turns out, Sky, that your dead friend Mr Jimmy Johnston took the role in Mrs Turner's murder. DNA and fingerprints have proven this. A few strands of his hair was found under her first fingernail by the pathologist. Tests carried out prove they were his hairs, almost certainly from her attacking him back. Then we found his fingerprints all over her bedroom furniture. But, we are bewildered by the lack of evidence in relation to him getting in and out as there are clearly no signs of forced entry'.

'Maybe he hid in her loft for a couple of months, killed her, then chipped after the area was clear. Did you check her loft? And by the way, he isn't my fucking dead friend'.

'Every area was checked, Sky, with a fine-toothed comb by the crime scene investigators. As I was saying no evidence was found that links to you, nothing whatsoever. Police had to break in to get to her. Nothing at all was touched outside her bedroom. The entire inside and outside of the house was examined. It's as if he never entered or left the house. Therefore, I was hoping that maybe you could bring some light to this; the pair did not even know of each other, Sky, we predict.'

'So what are you saying, they had to know each other for him to kill her? And maybe he wasn't actually there when this mastered act took place', Sky quizzed.

'That is not what I'm saying, no, I'm clearly stating the fact to you that no one broke in to that house that night, Sky. The whole house was locked; all windows closed, nothing broke or smashed, as I said, no forced entry. But because you say you knew the pair, and information shows you did, could you tell me something about the twosome, like did they come into contact? Or even the fact of knowing his plot against her would help us. You could let us in on what you know. Maybe you also know who killed Jimmy and Tina. Come on, Sky, I know you know who did this. Who are you trying to protect, is it really worth it? You will be charged on the grounds of perverting the course of justice and maybe even first-degree murder. Is it worth it'?

'Firstly, Miss Jenkins, if I was to be charged, and I won't be, I would plea on the grounds of diminished responsibility. I have a mental record as long as my arm, I'm fucking off my head. Hey, I will stay in a mental hospital…so fucking what? Secondly, Miss Jenkins, how do you know Jimmy's plot wasn't my bloody plot? I am the one that should take the full credit here and certainly not bloody Jimmy. Do not make me laugh'.

'Well, anything you could tell me, Sky, will of course help, but we know it wasn't you. It was not your fingerprints or DNA and your uncanny story does not fit in, but you know that I definitely know that you know something'.

'You haven't a clue, do you, so that's why you persist to pester me about it all'.

'Cut the crap, Sky, you were at the murder scene of Tina's, we know they're all linked in some way. Tina and Jimmy knew of each other and you knew all three'.

Lucy in a way felt sorry for Sky after reading her profile, but she could not work out their links, or could it all be just a coincidence? Lucy in the back of her mind knew the cases linked, but how?

'Well, if you read my statements properly that I did already with the police you would see clearly what I have said all along. I killed them. Read the statements again, then maybe it will become clearer to you, Miss Jenkins', Sky answered.

'I have and more than once, but no it's not clear. Why don't you tell me and make it clear'.

* * *

Sky could see her frustration, but Sky for the first time in being there felt comfortable with someone, having someone to talk to, even though this wasn't the subject she would have picked, but still, she started to enjoy Lucy's company.

'I suppose I could tell you about some things. I have never told anyone about things before, even if it's just for your entertainment because I know you're not a believer, but still, I could tell you'.

'Tell me what, Sky, a believer in what'? Lucy all of a sudden seemed very interested.

'What would you say if I said that my dreams are more than just dreams, and that they can make things real in reality that we're in'? Sky looked on for a reply to her comment, while her palms filled with sweated pleasure. The heat in that room was tight and the air went only in and out from their mouths around the room and back in again.

'I would say you're very delusional, Sky, but also I would say that I don't fully understand your statement'.

'Well, if I said that I dreamt the killings and made them reality, and that I had the power to work my magic in mysterious ways that wasn't clear to the visible eye'.

Sky continued as Lucy laughed.

'I would say impossible'.

'Nothing is impossible, Miss Jenkins, far from it. Why don't you open your mind and cross the parallel lines that are in front of you? Once you have crossed then maybe you'll see. Those fine lines are not the same as reality. If you cross them, then the other side will allow you to see, will allow you to want to see'.

'Sky, what are you going on about?

'I'm on about when I dream I cross to the other side, I cross to a place where I control what happens. If I want Mrs Turner dead, then so be it, it doesn't have to come down to Jimmy. In fact poor Jimmy didn't even know what was going on and he was nowhere near Mrs Turner when she passed to the other side. Mrs Turner unfortunately died alone, all alone, passing the fine lines before her. No one was there in her room that night...Lucy'.

Startled, Lucy wondered how she knew her first name. She asked, 'And what makes you think my name's Lucy'?

'Well, is it'? Sky leaned forward fast, making Lucy very nervous.

'Yes, it is'.

'Good guess then...you would think'. Laughing in a mocking manner, Sky crossed her left leg over her right and fell back into her white plastic chair, arms hanging over the sides.

'Look, Lucy, Miss Jenkins, whatever, let me tell you what. Why don't you run along and think about what I have said, and then get back to me. And while you're at it, don't you think it's time I was taken out of that room and treated correctly? You would think I was mad by the way you and your pals have been treating me'.

Sky half smiled to Lucy as Lucy was taken off guard by her comments, but she agreed it was time she was placed within a wing suitable for her needs.

'I will see what I can do, but in return, you will talk to me so I can understand you more...tomorrow, when we meet again, okay'?

'Whatever'. Sky did not hold her breath about being moved. She placed her head into her hands and started to think about Miss Tina Robson.

YOU'VE BEEN FRAMED

Evening of 16th March 2002, 11.20 p.m. Silence strikes the house of Miss pick-on-me-please Tina Robson. Sky squats on a branch of a tree, outside Tina's window, and waits for the time to hit 11.30 p.m. on her wristwatch. Five hours ago, Tina's parents left their home on time as Sky successfully planned. Sky conjured up this whole evening last night as she lay and dreamt...it would be a perfect night. Tina's parents are not due back until tomorrow night. Tonight the bitch belongs to Sky.

Tina sits quietly at her bedside table, brushing her brown-streaked hair, gazing at her reflection, at her beauty. So unaware, so safe...she feels. Sky looks on and can see through the window, such ugliness.

Her watch slowly hits 11.25 p.m. and the excitement is getting uncontrollable, she wants to bang on her window; she wants to show her presence. Her eyes trail Tina as she walks over to her bed and throws herself onto it. Kicking off the top cover with her feet, it falls with precision to the floor. Her head drops to the centre of the pillow. She shifts around to get her firm body into a snug position. She dozes, leaving the light on. Time hits 11.29 p.m. Sky still looks on through the window. In the darkness outside, the stars above Sky's head shine an unnatural glow. Sky smiles...it has started.

On the same wall as Tina's bedroom-door exit, next to her large coloured bubble lamp, sits a sleek wooden designer four-drawer chest and matching wardrobe. The bottom drawer opens. Out from the bottom drawer floats something black, a lace material with black ribbon tie-ups. The bottom drawer holds Tina's underwear in a colour-coded order. The floating black material was her thong. The thong tiptoed the air above Tina's head and then stopped.

Again from the same drawer a pair of fishnet tights glided through the air and fell softly to her bed. The tights slid under her legs, down near to her ankles, waiting for an evil command. Another pair did the same as the first pair; this time the tights lay across her stomach slowly, then started to shift under each hand at the wrists. Sky watches the magic she made, she does not miss a thing. Time hits 11.30 p.m.

The fishnet tights twist and knot fast around Tina's ankles and wrists, tightly, as if a pair of killing hands strangle at a victim's neck, choking, holding, squeezing. Tina awoke from her slight daze, ready to scream aloud. The black thongs fell, as if a brick fell, into her wide mouth. Gagged and bounded, her eyes filled with tears. Forcefully rolling off her bed, she crashed to the floor, banging her head. Tina could not run nor cry for help. Sky was winning.

A dark shadow crept around the bedroom and the room grew faint. Tina got to her knees and headed for the door, shuffling, but her murmured sounds of help could not be heard. The lampshade by her bed lifted at a hurried speed and smashed at her skull repeatedly. She fell. Tina was out for the count, as the lampshade continued to beat. Tina's cataleptic body moved around while an invisible strength slammed each bone in her body. Blood visible, deep red blood dribbled from the broken flesh, then the dribbles turned into a gush of spray. From outside, Sky banged at the window, her lips moving to the words, 'Die, Tina'. Sky climbed down the tree, jumped to the ground and walked off.

Inside the bedroom an evil takes over, a dark evil with a customised plan. A plan to kill, a plan that had already met with others and killed. The unseen evil swiftly raises Tina's bound legs into the air, her body jerks still. Her knickers are tugged at, pulled down over her knees; they take a pew just above her ankles, her nightdress violently ripped open. The evil rapes her. Sky sits upon a wobbly fence. She smiles....

SHOOT THE BUZZING OLD GIRL

Sky moved to an open wing, as Lucy promised her. Security was tight, like a pair of old jeans that no longer fitted because you stuffed yourself with cream cakes and you couldn't even squeeze your bum into them any more, which meant there was no way of Sky escaping, just like there was no way of you doing that zip up.

Sky settled in just fine because she now had a soft warm bed, better than the one she just left. Having a better bed meant a lot to her, it was her home.

Sitting in the open area that they called the living area, everything in sight was of imitation material. Plastic furniture all placed in identical squares around the room, ten tables with four chairs and four plastic place mats to each. The picture frames looked like dark wood, but were not. You could see a thin peeling layer of paint and grain that gave this effect with herbs and spices as pictures, hanging against the wall that once was white but now stale yellow.

Two doors insight, one fire door for emergencies to go down the stairwell, in case of fire, and the other leads from out the living area into the sleeping zone. For these inpatients there was nowhere to run.

All doors locked at all times. At the back of the living area there is a nurses desk and work area hidden behind tall glass, one side opens up to allow the nurses to talk with the inpatients or to hand out daily medicine. You can't see the corner hidden by the nurses desk unless you're up close, that corner leads in to a big hall, where meals were served. This room hosted a few chores for the inpatients. The first wall in this room held the chores list for them to stick to each day and changes each month, so no one felt they have been mistreated and overworked. All the walls were of dark blue tiles with dirty grout. A large stainless-steel two-way sink and an oven, electric for safety reasons. Lots of cupboard space under lock and key…so no one decides to stick a knife into someone else or eats all the food…here there is always 24/7 supervision. A white fire alarm stuck to the ceiling twenty feet away from the broken ceiling fan. A long crack goes from one side of the wall over the ceiling to the other. It looks clean, tidy, and pleasant in this ward.

In this ward, priority is based on the hygiene levels and the standard is high. Every day a nurse will check individually, making sure it is finished to perfection. Anyone slacking will have a warning and a second warning will lead to having extras removed.

The only thing needed for this ward was a makeover, fresh new paints and curtains with new pictures and carpets, and while they're at it they should get that ceiling fan fixed. All the same, the lack of funds that drift into this hospital is stiff, hence the ten-year gap when the decorators were last in.

If you come back out from the kitchen and look the opposite way you will see two doors with black stickers, indicating which room is for whom. These two rooms hold the toilets and washing area with a bath and two showers in each. These rooms are clean but today the men's room has a water leak. On the other hand was that Mr Jones who stuck recycled tissue in the sinks and leaving the cold water tap running while he was pissing all around the floor and toilet seat as he left with a sly grin across his gummed mouth.

Sky was playing with a pack of cards and in front of her making buzzing noises was an old purple rinse-haired woman. She did not seem to irritate Sky at the start. Sky quite enjoyed the attention she got from being the "new person" and all. It would not last though; there were new people, so-called freaks, coming in and out all the time, like a conveyer belt shifting them in by the dozen.

Only a handful ever got the certificate certifying them of being sane and being able to return to the hellhole they came from. Like a special offer in a shop: buy one out-of-date freak and get the other one free.

'Buzz buzz, why are you here buzz buzz', the old woman inquired.

'Never you mind', Sky responded, smiling back at her. For the first time, Sky felt settled.

'Buzz buzz, I'm here too, buzz buzz'. Sky looked at her as if to say, yes I realize this fact, I can see you.

'Why are you here'? Sky asked in return. The old woman smiled back as if copying.

'Buzz buzz, why are you here, buzz buzz'. Sky's eyebrows rose.

'I just told you there's no reason, and if I did tell you, I would have to kill you '.

'Buzz buzz, I just told you there's no reason, buzz buzz', the old woman repeated.

'Please stop buzzing and repeating now, it's getting on my pip'.

'Buzz buzz, please stop, you're getting on my pip, buzz buzz'.

Sky sat up in a tall position and looked hard at her while crossing her arms. She didn't want to upset the buzzing old woman, but she was driving Sky crazy by now.

'Could you please buzz somewhere else? I'm trying to play cards here, can't you see this'?

'Buzz buzz, can't you see this, I'm here too, buzz buzz'. The old girl sat looking then she suddenly started to clap with no control over her old and most likely very experienced hands.

'WOULD YOU...please stop'! Sky shouted, but then by the time half the sentence was over, she whispered the end, because she did not want to make a scene, especially not now she had found something secure.

'Buzz buzz, would you please stop, you're getting on my pip. I'm here too, can't you see this, buzz buzz'. Still she smiled away, not knowing of the harm she was doing.

'Fucking BUZZ off will you, you stupid old bat'! Sky stood to her feet fast waiting for the old girl to get the hint and shift her wrinkly purple hair-rinsed body away. The old girl stood too. They engaged eye contact for a few moments.

'Buzz buzz, buzz buzz'. The old buzzing girl then walked off, looking back every now and again. 'Buzz buzz, I will have to kill you, buzz buzz'.

Sky could still hear it; she placed her hands over her ears and sat back down with her elbows on the white plastic table looking down at the joker card.

The old girl had left her cigarettes on the table with a lightup lighter that also played "Auld Lang Syne." Sky flipped the lip open, pulled out a cigarette, burnt the end and she puffed that fag like there was no tomorrow. She had forgotten how a fag tasted, her head receiving the whirls. Then again, she longed quietly for a quick dab of speed or a toke on a joint to even a quick session on her crack pipe.

Sky was able to control her clucking for any drug, having control and being like your typical casual user. She often went on long periods of being clean so it did not affect her like some she had seen in her past. As long as she had her dreams, she felt full of total contempt.

While Sky sat, she drifted back to her past days of when she was around eight, when she started to fully understand the drug world even though she choked on her first joint at age seven. She had decided to herself at that age, whether it was true or not, from what she had seen and learnt the meaning of taking drugs was more on the reasoning than from boredom. The addiction came second, never first....

* * *

I saw it as how can you be addicted to anything if you have not tried it or known it? To try it, you were most likely bored, than it being forced upon oneself. I saw many bored creepy crawlies prowl about my territory before and after their signing on days to receive a giro to pay for their addiction or thieving to destroying someone's property. Selling their hot goods at knock-down prices and to my parents even lower, but alternatively I could fully grasp the fact of why they did it, but that does not mean I thought it was right.

In a couple of hours' work, they could have made more than a working man in one week. In a couple hours' work they had enough for their compulsion. In a couple of hours' work, they could chill knowing they were high until the next dawn showed itself.

To work is hard, to be accepted was even harder, never mind in many cases that I had seen at my home, that none having much of an education. That is where the influence came that woke me up inside, to make sure I stuck to my schooling and not to be like them.

The so-called poor in the world are looked at as poor excuses for humans, but then I would rather be that poor excuse of a human than be born with a silver spoon in my mouth. That was also half my problem at school, not always being standard to everyone else's labels. But turns out I was one of the cleverest and that satisfied me more than those tormenters will ever know. Still, being poor has no credit you're never going to be anything in life, hence the 'pushers lounge' at my house. If you did become something then was it just pure luck? The girls getting pregnant just for a roof over their heads, these easily given to them by the local council after being kicked out from the family home. Parents still claiming monies as if they were still living there. The girls, only babies themselves, having babies they cannot even look after. Finding the house they had always dreamed of turns out they could not even keep it clean. Furnishing it was next on the list but from lack of resources, they could not, so their partners went on the pinch to please their girls. This world is a vicious loop that only comes back around to bite you on your fat behind....

* * *

Sky never wanted to be like that, she wanted to be special and she knew she was special. To Sky, Lucy's child would have been classed as 'normal' due to her having and will to come have everything in life. Just 'normal', nothing more, nothing less, and never knowing or learning what Sky's meaning of special meant. Now to be special was to be different and to be different you needed continuous tasks that you faced in your life. Being on your own and overcoming those tasks that you hurdle to mould you into a special person and not to be helped all through your life, not learning to stand on your own two feet, is the first route to a breakdown. To be special is to acknowledge what life has offered you and to make the most of it and not complain, but only to better yourself and to better yourself in this life was hard.

Therefore, Sky knew what life had offered her, the gift she dreamt then of course, she had to use to its full expectations, and she was. She knew that the dreams were trying to cleanse the hate she had for the normal. The victims she murdered were normal to Sky. They were the ones who had everything they ever wanted but tried to take everyone else's something. Be it monies or taking one's dignity, it was all one and the same because of one thing: it never belonged to the normal in the first place to take. Sky hated the normal, she hated her parents, and she hated the 'pushers lounge'.

Sky even hated her time spent at her auntie's. Everyone painted a pretty picture, but truly, Sky's auntie was just a tamer version of her mother's ways. She would pretend she cared, she pretended to even help at the meetings they had with the doctors. After telling them of how much she cared and would help Sky overcome her problems, as soon as they arrived back home she was right back out the door, never seeing her for days at a time.

Sky felt as if she were safer being at home within the 'pushers lounge'. At least she was used to that emptiness and being alone feeling, she felt even worse at her aunties. Sky never understood why she had to leave her home in the first place.

The worst days she encountered were of her schooling at sixteen; as adolescence kicked in, it made things inferior. This was the year she was picked on the most out of any other year. As well as her stringy, sticky white gum attack that made the icing on the cake, Tina also did other mean things to Sky. Tina used to trip her up in the dinner hall, food going everywhere in front of everyone. Tina used to take her bag and hide or burn it, and with the help of her mates, they kicked Sky in after school in the field nearby.

Also that year, Sky had met a lad her own age. He was a loner, he did not do school but was highly gifted. All the girls liked him. He lived, when he was around, in the local area, but he had no home and vanished from time to time. He would play guitar for money sitting on the street curbs or local town doorways. A beautiful voice he had, with hidden darkness that only showed itself via his chorus. A stunning performance he would always share with his public when they stood viewing his raw talent; by throwing money into his black cap they showed appreciation.

The pair, in their quality time shared, would split secrets of their past and exchange witchcraft spells, but Sky did most of the exchanging. To her surprise, they had a lot in common. He was her first love. Her first night of passion was with him under the moonlight, and that night she would never forget. Her first love soon became her quickest love. Nothing lasted for Sky. Even though later on in their strange relationship he did her wrong, something so wrong, he then just simply became one more in line on her list to kill. Sky knew what he had done to her was under Tina's influence, but still, can you push that aside and forgive or deep down did he really know right from wrong? If he loved her liked he had said, then he would never have done it. Out of all the pain caused to Sky, his stung the most. His prick went deeper down inside than any other prick. His prick pieced her heart in two. His sharp prick left a huge hole that could never fill with love again.

* * *

'Hello, how are you, Sky'? Lucy had been calling her name for the last five minutes, but Sky was still deep in thought, still head in hands looking downward at that joker card.

'Sky, are you okay'? Lucy said again.

Her cigarette had burnt away still in her fingers. Sky's mind could wander to all stages of her past. Sky's mind was a powerful tool that someone needed to examine.

Lucy pulled the chair next to her and sat waiting for her acknowledgement. Sky, still with her hands over her ears, twisted her head around facing to Lucy. Giving Lucy a dirty look, she then turned her head back to its original position. 'Buzz buzz', she mumbled, and once again, she drifted away from normal reality, deep down into her subconsciousness, away from what was real and to her recalls, a cock-and-bull story....

* * *

Sitting on a small unclean Hopper 'n Stopper bus, I was heading back to my auntie's. At the back, I sat gawking from out the window. I was waiting for the next line of people to pay and get on. Old people mostly with their travel permits ready in their hands, because they have reached the sixty-five-age period and were entitled to so much off the full bus fare. With their old-fashioned clothes and white clean cotton hair, I had total respect for this age group. Not that I would want to reach to that peak age of good old oldies, and the clickity click of the bingo hall.

As I sat and looked upon the experienced members of our so-called society, I realised they were not all like Mrs Turner, an old battleaxe. Moreover, it made me feel good to know that I had killed her and removed normal scum from our daily lives and that I was soon to remove more. I felt good for doing my bit for society.

In fact, the older members of society actually did me no wrong and this is why I had the respect I had for them.

I get so offended when reading a newspaper and seeing an older person being mugged and or killed for bloody money, it makes me sick.... It makes me hate.

I respect the older person because they are so friendly and calm; they give you that sense of freedom and non-caring for much other than what really matters. What their past could have encountered and how they managed to live through all the dramatic changes of life they lead and are now seeing changes for the worst. It makes you wonder how they did it.

On this bus, I can see clearly that the older persons had inherited from their creators old traditions; they had the sticker stuck to their heads. On this bus, I can see clearly that the young ones were different. We do not see this old tradition pushed into the young; they wear a different breed of sticker.

Maybe it is due to the time that passes us all, it shows to the older persons exactly what real value is. On the other hand, maybe it is due to this new generation, the young, that shows to them time means nothing and that old tradition has gone.

However, still I could never live that old, be it the hard decision on a pink or purple hair rinse or the fact that when you reach this age you're put on the shelf and whatever you were has merely disappeared. You're scared to wander at a late time along a path that once was your own safe haven or the knowing of the left unlocked back door is now never safe; not in this lifetime will it ever be like that again.

I do not like or respect much but fair play to the older people in this messed-up place. As for Mrs Turner, well, what can I say, she was a nasty piece of work, I had no choice but to kill her. Normal, as I say, I hate the fucking normal. She was an old battleaxe for sure. Then there is more scum that physically drains me. There is Jimmy, the racist paint-spraying twat, his anti-this-and-that attitude of an uneducated boy. And Tina, well, what a whore, a selfish me, me, me bitch. Then there is death to come, there's Adam, a lying using shit that makes my blood curdle. I lost my virginity to that shit, I can't get over it.

They were normal. I am trying to remove the normal to allow us special people to breathe. They each had their own reasons to die; they each had the normal manner of scum and their actions. They were individual victims but very much the same specimen, which turns my insides out. Normal insignificant fools.

I tell you all something; if I had the time, I would do this motherland a favour and remove a hell of a lot more normal scum. I would use my power to destroy the racists, child abusers, anti gays and the terrorists. I would bring back hanging and stoning to death, for the enjoyment for us all to see. I would love to see hippies collaborate a new government of your typical 'Yer, peace man' sayings and banners. I would like to see the so-called high people in the regime of the world stuffed and put on display. Then to finally call the UN in for peace crack pipe sessions, and to discuss love and not war, but to only convey the destruction of pain to the non-believers and to their self-righteous values and their deliverance of devastation and hate to this world they choose to bring.

People will assume I'm wrong in thinking this but truly, I only think in what I believe, and that is simply removing those that affect others and me. They have their rights and I have mine. If they choose to plant bombs or shoot and stab gays or abuse children and mug the old, then as sick as it is and they seem to believe that it is their right...well blow me down if I feel the urge to kill them.

In fact, the harm I could be doing to those bastards is not even close to the harm they are dishing out. I know I need to get rid of more but I can't, as much as I would love to, and it's not that I do not have the power because I do, but my time is running out fast. The thing is, I just do not have the time. So therefore, I am only attacking those close to me, those that hurt me, those that turned me into this special person and gave me the will to invite my power to realisation. I wish so much that I never gave my virginity *away to that cheap trick Adam. I cannot get it from out of my mind.*

The bus stopped again and on walked a young man wearing dark blue tracksuit bottoms and matching top. He stood for ages at the top of the bus, paying for his ticket. The bus driver was helping him with his wallet, taking out the loose coins. Everyone was getting irritated over the long wait. The young man then walked up the bus, passing others with an insecure look upon his guiltless face. Everyone he passed, you heard a long gasp, they were staring hard at him, at his hands. His hands were different than ours, only fists of pale white flesh with the thumb fingers and baby fingers bending awkward, pointing a way that was not normal to the so-called normal person. He slowly sat next to me but I did not mind. Everyone turned and stared; acting like they were staring at something else, but clearly it was his hands that amused their small minds.

I could not believe that the members of this bus had so little respect, such an annoying presence he must have felt. I guess he has had an annoying presence stalk him all his life. Maybe I felt uneasy and not him, maybe it was I feeling ridiculed and watched.

From the corner of my eye, I saw him, and not because I was watching in the same manner as the others chose to, trying to hide his hands. I felt a guilty sensation rock my insides on behalf of everyone sitting on this bus. I saw his hands were contorted and stiff. They looked like hooks, shaking, knobbly, white pale hooks.

Continually others turned to look and he continued to hide away in shame. I did not feel sorry for him but for them. I pitied them. I turned and looked him in the eye and not at his deformed hands and I smiled to him. And past those deformed features, his smile shined back, a smile I will never forget.

My stop was coming up and I stood, shuffled past him, and knelt down next to the seat we shared. I decided to whisper to him and inside I hoped he did not feel like I was patronising him, as I was not. I am not superior to anyone else, especially not him. So instead, I decided to shout my whisper to him for all to hear. I wanted him to feel more superior to them including me. 'You're special, you're like me, and do not let anyone tell you any different. Do not hide the person that you are...ever'. His eyes watered but he smiled again and I left the bus.

The lesson I learnt days after the bus journey was that we are all victims for reasons we never created. We are all victims of god's creation. However, we are told by high society that we are equal, free and even, and we all try to live by this rule...what a load of fucking bullshit. We are force fed to believe we have rights but we have nothing. We live under their rule, we live unfair.

Brutality is in all our genes, we all have a nasty bone but for individual reasons. The young man I met on that bus that day with the smile that shined was found dead. He was dead because a group of younger boys let their inborn brutality stick knives into him, because they did not understand why a freak walked their walk. Why a freak breathed the same air they breathed. How a freak was ever created in the first place. What did he do to them? Why him? Just remember that this is the same young man who was scared by a busload of people, the same young man who said nothing on this journey, he only hid his deformed curse because of the evil looks that surrounded him. How I pity you all....

ADAM, OOH, ADAM, YOU SHOULDN'T HAVE

A running stream split the woods in two. Wind breezes shuffled in and out from the branches. Sky and Adam were getting ready for a chanted love spell with an expectation from each other that tonight they would become one. Their first night together had to be right. Helping their imagination was her trustworthy friend, LSD. Black beeswax candles half burned within their homemade camp built from branches swung together. A torn chequered blanket beneath their bodies as they knelt within a trance they had fixed amid themselves.

To them this was being romantic in an adult manner but little did they know what romantce really was. Sky dressed in a long black robe, Adam unaware of her black sexy underwear hidden away from sight. He wore his army jacket and blue jeans with his half-grown blonde dreads blending in with his ghostly white skin, from lack of sunlight even existing in his daily routine. He was in a hideaway, not very sociable Count Dracula style hard rock, laid-back kind of male. This was most likely the reason for the appearance and attitude he carried. Her hair was delicately placed, pulled into a sexy twisted design with black curls draping down from her sides with stunning dark makeup. She was pleased with her results, dressed to impress.

Adam was more into the drug side of life than the paranormal that longed from Sky. He declared he had once experimented in a drunken foolish ceremony with his mates one evening and little did Sky know was how badly wrong it went. Nevertheless, he still made out to Sky that he was an expert, but he never showed her his claims. Sky was in love, she did not really care that he used her to get the drugs for him, and being free, what else could he do but exploit her? She did not even care if he did really have any clue about witchcraft or if he even ever really heard of it or knew of its meanings. She had found someone she loved for the first time and believed for the first time that someone actually loved her back. In a way he did, in a way he wanted to, but typically, he could love her today and love miss's thingamajig tomorrow.

Sky did not worship the devil, nor did she sacrifice animals to demons. She was still a learner in a sense; still intrigued from the years she had involved herself in witchcraft. It was not out of harm, at first, but of self-learning and the power to create ointments and spells for every notion. One she planned to use that night was one she had known but never used. She came fully prepared with her charms. She chose the perfect evening being a Friday, with planet Venus oozing with love and attraction. Her belongings sat beside her ready for this spell-crafting showdown, oils and herbs, a bag of red candles, natural ones, and a pack of fresh pins within a small black coloured wool bag. With her instinct and visualization in place, she was more than ready to lose her virginity her way. To her this was the right way.

On her wrist and in her ears, around her neck and on her two middle fingers, she wore sapphire crystals to represent the month, the moonlit Friday night of September. Placing the thirteen red candles between them in a line, she passed the wool bag over to him to expose two pins. She could not touch his fresh pin and he with hers. He took one out and pasted it back. She then handed him the first candle and she took the thirteenth. They both started scratching in each other's names and the words 'lust' and 'love'. Swapping them back over, the pair signed each other's candle. A signature of love and blessing was the meaning.

Then she placed the thirteenth candle into the first position and he placed the first into the thirteenth position. Leaning over, they kissed a long kiss of sealing. She then took his hand and from behind her pulled out a black-handled, double-edged dagger and slit across his inner hand, leading the blood into the chalice. These two were used together to signify sexual mixing. She then slit her own hand on the outer side and drops fell once again to the chalice. Half the service was over.

Pulling out her lighter, she asked him to light the candles, but to leave one and thirteen. He did so as she chanted her magical words. Sky then blew out all the lit candles. Guiding his hand to hers, they walked into the fresh cold air standing face to face under the moonlight. Sky dropped her robe, showing him of her full figure and sex appeal; he soaked it all up in desire. She then placed the dagger to her feet after making a line with it in the ground to keep away the bad. The tensions being released were wild, they entwined their passion around their bodies. The heat flushed out from their flesh and the brilliant sensual exterior of the two caressed in beat. The bonding for the new was from out of this world; the pair had now become one.

When they finally finished their sexual experience, she left him lying completely happy and fulfilled. After picking up the dagger, she headed back to the homemade camp. Walking around the line in the ground and not over it, she entered. Sky burnt up the first and thirteenth candle, then kneeling in front of them, she drank from the chalice a few drops. She licked around her lips covering them in blood; she then licked the dagger. She blew out the candles that were burning. She had completed the final part and she felt satisfaction from her ritual, she felt full.

Successful evening or not or did he come up to scratch that night would be the question, but one question that Sky could not answer having nothing to compare him to. Therefore, being satisfied with the beauty that they swapped, they both were pleased. Whether it was the drug's participation that made it complete and the spell chanting, than his manly style, she guessed they played a huge part in the service.

That night she had sold her rights to him believing he was the one and exchanging bodily fluids, she had now become a woman, his woman. After her changing event, they carried on frequently with their meetings, rituals, and drug takings. They became very close and she was blinded from the love. Still, little did she know then of his life of imitation.

PERSONALLY, I BLAME THE PARENTS

Time had moved on from the buzzing old girl experience. Sky ate corn on the cob with bruised boiled potatoes and slices of lamb smothered in thick gravy. Prodding her fork from lack of appetite, she watched taking in her company's bad manners. The food was atrocious even though it sounded pleasant when she first saw it written on the menu and ticked for it. She decided that this was maybe the right time to go on a hunger or work strike, knowing her stay there was going to be an even longer one than hoped.

In front of her was a man with light brown receding hair flicked to one side, a pointy nose and a pair of slim lips. He looked a bit like an outdated teacher suited and booted, but without the boots. He did not believe in boots, shoes, or anything that covered the feet. He believed god walked the earth barefooted and therefore so should he. Sinners wore covered-up materials. If he had his way as he did in the public or tried, he would be sitting in front of all of them naked, and that in itself would put Sky off her food for a week.

Sky watched his little pinkie push outwards as he lifted and sipped at his tea. She could only appreciate his fine lines on his face that showed years of hard work, misery, love, hate, and of course madness. For what, why do we do it? All those lines showed his life, and for what, to end up in a fucking loony bin. The poor sod has most likely realised by now that the life he once led has turned out to be nothing but a bloody waste of time. Life itself all summed up upon a man's features. A good read from a human book. There was nothing sexier than a man with his experience.

Next to her was this young person, Sky knew her as Mary-Anna, and she did not even look like she had one mad bone in her body. Until she stood and started to empty the ashtrays into her pockets and started drinking from the leftover cups when she had her own to drink from. Sky started to laugh aloud to herself in bewilderment but not wanting to upset anyone. The next thing Sky knew, she was burning from hot tea which Mary-Anna had thrown all over her.

'What the hell was that for'? Sky yelled in agony. Standing up fast, Sky pushed at the woman hard. The woman stepped back and pointed her finger in Sky's face.

'What you finding funny, hey? Laugh at me, I teach you lesson, you whore bag', the young woman splattered back with a strange accent, still waggling the first finger.

'I was laughing aloud but not at you. Whore bag, you say, but not as good as your mummy am I, selling her muffin like a rotten fruitcake. I bet you take after your mummy, huh? You silly slag. Go wash, you stink'. Sky winked.

The pair started to fight in front of everyone. Every nutter in that room jumped up from shock; at last there was some excitement for them. The young woman grabbed Sky's hair while trying to bite at her. Sky punched Mary-Anna into the stomach and effortlessly rushed her hands up to grab Mary-Anna's head and heatedly bringing it back down to meet Sky's knee. The young woman fell to the ground.

'No more, I say, no more. Do not hate, do stop', she squeaked, pushing her arms out to stop Sky. As the cheering surrounded Sky the rush started to fill her system. She was now seeing blurs and hearing voices. Sky's visions changed, she now saw Tina lying before her and what a turn around this was for Sky. Tina being beaten by her was a remarkable achievement. Kicking and stamping on the poor young woman's back, not realising her delusion.

'Look who it is, miss pick on me please'! Sky yelled. 'Not laughing now, are you, Tina'? Sky jumped on to Mary-Anna's front and took her ears and banged then lifted, then banged then lifted that head up and down, to and from that solid floor.

'Get her, go on, stick one in, anyone want to bet £10, come on, anyone'? shouted a man, an ex-gambler by the sound of him jumping up and down, his head bobbing at the back of the crowd. Sky could not stop, she was letting her tensions run wild. Still head banging away with someone else's head, she then focused on the blood. Sky started to slow herself down. Seeing Tina and Mary-Anna's images mix together, she stopped. There was blood on her hands and the girl was not moving. Without turning, Sky looked out from the corner of her eyes and noticed the crowd. Looking back down she saw the young woman who had a habit of emptying ashtrays into her pocket but it wasn't Tina.

'Oh shit '. Sky numbly pulled herself off Mary-Anna's body. 'I'm so sorry'. She wiped her black locks from her face as hairs stuck to the warm blood. Sky looked around again and she saw the long white coats heading her way. Her demons.

'It wasn't my fault'! Sky cried pointing to the unconscious Mary-Anna.

'I did not mean to hurt her. Will she be okay? Have I killed her?' Those white coats, three of them, leaped onto Sky, holding her tight and taking her away. To a recognizable room with her arms pulled behind her back, Sky knew where she was heading. It was Sky's old room. For another lonely night, she faced.

'I did not mean it. I could not help it. Tell her sorry'. Sky allowed them to remove her from the only place that had normality, where she felt protected. The crowd started to dissemble but from the odd few still shouted with enthusiasm.

She was thrown head first into the white padded cell. Now with the white straight jacket back on, Sky rolled to the corner. 'Tell her sorry. Tell her shit happens and that this is life. Please someone tell her that what goes around comes around. Surely she will understand that'. Sky flopped to the floor motionless and she closed her eyes while violently banging her head. She never wanted to hurt anyone but her list of hated, only her so-called normal enemies. She felt guilty for this, but the rush still enormous flowing around her veins, Sky had just wished it were Tina she had hurt and not Mary-Anna. The slamming of the door once again hammered about her mind as the high dose of Valium injection they gave her dominated her system. After awhile her head had stopped bashing, and her mind drifted once again....

* * *

'Mum, can I borrow some money please'? Sky asked her phoney mother when she was eleven. She needed school dinner money and this she had to ask for on a daily basis, but most times Sky went without. Sky waited for a reply as her mother was applying frosted pink lippy. 'Mum, could I please'? again, she asked. 'Where's your father, go ask him and piss off, shut the door on your way out'. Sky's face dropped as she turned away from the female she called mum.

Heading down the staircase, she heard whispers. She stopped and sat on the blue carpet with her pigtails carefully in place and listened.

'What you on about it won't come to that, Kim'?

'How can you say that, I mean, how long's it been now, what, a month? Come on, Jacob, wake up. People are going to get hurt if you do not pay up. The East boys do not like being treated like fucking mugs, you know this'. Sky

tried to hear all their words.

'Look, I'm sorting it, it's only a few thousand, I deal with it. Just get off my case and grab me that pipe, will you'.

It turned silent. Sky realised it was once again about drug debts. She skipped for the front door swinging her arm out to catch the lonely school bag for the lonely child, knowing there was no point asking for dinner money. He was broke, why be a pest to him? Sky slammed the door behind her, knowing her tummy was not going to be fed that day.

Walking home slowly after a long day at school and having nothing to rush back to, after-school hours dragged for Sky. She wished so much that she could just go and live in a boarding school, at least that would be like getting a ready-made family that she could interact with. She had no company, unless she sat with the normal scum in the 'pushers lounge', but she could not keep up with all the different faces each day.

When she finally returned home, she entered and everything was normal when she stuck her head around into the 'pushers lounge'. The unforgettable stink swooped up her nostrils.

'Hi, it's only me', Sky informed.

No reply was returned, this being a customary welcome. She hovered toward the kitchen, dropped her school bag onto the floor and she took a pot noodle from the cupboard. She switched on two electric controls, one for the kettle and one for the CD player. She threw her black school blazer to the chair and pressed number seven on the sliver Sony four-disc player, that being her favourite song on the disc, Nirvana In Utero, 'Very Ape'.

As she waited for the kettle, she pulled out her two thick brown elastic hair bands and shook her black hair to unravel the pigtails. As the tune started to kick in with the sounds of the electric guitar, she looked like a high rock chick. Sky started to sing.

'I am buried up to my neck in contradictionary lies, I take pride as the king of illliterature, I'm very ape and very nice'. Sky moved slowly all around the kitchen to the song's beat, now shouting the words with an insufferable meaning, She screamed.

Seeing the kettle's red light turn off, she walked to the direction the steam came from. Pouring in the boiling water to greet her noodles, she carried on shouting while still nodding away to the beat. 'Out of the ground, into the sky, out of the sky, into the dirt'.

Suddenly a huge bang made Sky fall to the floor, crawling fast under the kitchen table where she hid with her tail in between her legs, just like the lost dog she had always known herself to be. Knocking the pot noodle with her, it fell smashing to the floor. The hot water expanded towards her ankles, wetting her white cotton socks. Under the table, Sky could not stop shaking.

'JACOB'.

Sky heard a gunshot...she could see only brief glimpses of movement in the other room from her hiding place.

'Jacob, it's the police! Chuck the crack down the fucking toilet'! Sally Shanti shouted. Sky's mother ran down the stairs not realising that stood before her husband was the East boy and it certainly was not the police. From under her corner of the table, Sky saw the bullet pierce her father's skull and enter his brain, exiting out the other side straight into the green painted peeling wall turned to a red fleck design. Everything was going so fast, it was to hard for Sally to take in, her husband dead before her.

Sally stood in shock. The East boy turned, he fired the gun, hitting her in the chest. Her facial expression was of a dying woman seeing her life flash before her, as if watching a flipbook. Soppy eyes that were saying, 'why me'? Her mouth took its last gasp of drug-smoked air. She fell in a sluggish movement in the hallway as Sky looked on from under the kitchen table, watching the body, like a ghoul fall to the floor.

Sky's bottom lip trembled from fear, her eyes so filled with revelations of bloodstained crime, her mother before her dead. The song still played loud but it was as if no one could hear it, like watching a silent movie. Sky whispered, 'No, please, God, no'.

She scattered quickly from under the table like a rat and crawled silently past her dead mother. With her mother's eyes still open and Sky feeling she was watching her every move, she was dead; the blinking had stopped. The pale pink-coloured jumper Sally wore now had a strange dark red pattern that slowly appeared to confirm she was shot in the heart area.

Trying hard not to be caught by the East boy, Sky slowly crept up the stairs. She was lucky the East boy was counting the money and collecting the drugs to even notice her. Then out walked Kim from the toilet, but being so out of her head, nearly on an overdose level, she did not have a clue why that magnum bullet smacked her in the forehead, just like Jacob, when entering the 'pushers lounge'. Besides, she will never tell the story, unlike Sky, hidden away now under her bed.

From fear of her life being taken and not from her parents' death she blubbered. After the commotion, the East boy left with everything that he came for. Hearing the car spin off, Sky went for the phone and dialed 999 and waited alone in deep shock pretending nothing had happened, singing, 'Here we go round the mulberry bush, the mulberry bush, on a cold an frosty morning'. All she could do was charge her parents for her torment. Sky personally blamed her parents....

* * *

Sky hated having to live in this corrupting manner. Sky hated seeing such craziness. Sky hated everyone and everything for her hardship. Sky's mind never stood still, it roamed to every nostalgia moment in no order, and it just played the flashbacks repeatedly around her brain box, while she questioned herself and answered herself in hush-hush.

No one else could get her to believe that she was not to blame, she was not to torment herself for her past, that her survival within this family tree was not of her own doing, and that one cannot predict what life has to offer. As sad a story as life can be, one thing to remember is that you can learn and continue to exist from it and better yourself without the excuses that some give for their actions. In addition, this is what Sky was learning and she is mastering. Her dreams, her evil magic, her deeds that she delivered were the only things that gave her a purpose. A purpose to destroy all that is wrong to her. Once her purpose was completed she would be at peace with her inner self, and she could then tell the tale of her marvel, she can move on to the gates that closed her from her paradise. As she heard not that long ago, darkly whispered inside of her: *"To end one's secret will mean to end you. To end you means you have succeeded"*.

Sky, still searching around through her sorrow, dashed around upstairs, lost and confused, which way should she turn, what story should she execute next. One minute she would be at her parents' deaths, the next at the scene of total deceit from a loved one. She continued to travel her misery, she continued to talk to herself and answer her many questions...

* * *

I was on my way to meet Adam, normal time and normal place as it has always been, but on this day, I was running a bit late. An edgy feeling already sweated over me as I was trotting through the woods about half a mile from our love nest, as we called it.

My backpack was heavy from a nice food supply, apples and ham rolls, scotch eggs, chicken salad and a bottle of whiskey...Adam's favourite, I frequently brought this with me. I smoked on a joint and double-checked my front jean pocket to see if it still contained the pot and speed for our proactive afternoon. It was still concealed around my waist area, safe as it were I then took another drag from my inhaling friend and I felt good, in fact, I was greatly missing the pants off my loved one. Last time I saw him was only four days ago but still, I was deeply in love. I needed a hit from him and his hit was better than any drug at this precise moment in my life. I just loved to stare at him, I loved his blonde, dreaded hair. I would twist it when we talked. I loved to talk with him. He would hear my words, and knowing that no one could come between us, it felt grand...so I thought.

In these woods, you could easily get lost if you did not know the way. It was very pretty, full of bluebells flowing wordlessly, but on other occasions being high, those bluebells spoke to me. Many a times now I walked this walk but never ever sang the song, the love song I now sing.

I was getting nearer and I was knackered, maybe I should have quit smoking, which was my New Year's resolution, as I dragged myself to the spot he awaited. Then the hard, sharp blood-sucking pinprick hit me. The pain was from on the outside of this world; my body physically fell to the floor as I looked ahead of me and saw them.

As I knelt on my knees, I felt the double-edged dagger slice me in two, the dagger we shared for the love I gave, just plunged cruelly into my heart. I could not even swallow, I was as 'dry as a camel's ass' that needed lubrication to help moisten my heart-breaking pain. My eyes swelled up with hate, my vision slowly drowned and sunlight flickered as I rubbed on them.

I slowly pulled my body by my hands, slowly across the branch-infested woodland floor, my fingertips snatching for that extra pull while sharp bits cut under my long freshly painted black nails. They...yes, that is the bit that shocked me, they being the word, it should have only been him. They...had not seen me, how could they, over their mouth sucking invasion they portrayed. As I watched on secretly I realised just who that other they was, but not to my surprise I guess it's who I guess it would have been if it was going to be anyone.

Once I took on board that image that cavorted with my first and only love, I knew that my life was now placed into a no-win situation. There was only one way to get even. Revenge is sweet. Time will come for them all, so I then left the scene and waited for my turn to come. Yet, nothing prepared me for what was to come after my sticky white gum attack. And yes, Tina was the one to play the role of sticking it into my hair, and to this day the pair still don't know what I saw, that draining day the pair shared.

They will never know about the views I took in. My silence echoed within me and I knew time would tell and show me the way, the icing on the cake was sure to follow and it did. For the pair of them to act as if nothing happened, for him to carry on seeing me, without a scratch of admiration to tell me about his act of deception. I knew I would get even, I was sure to fall on my feet. That night I removed sticky white gum and chanted my spell and wow, did I bounce off my feet....

QUESTION TIME

Two days passed since the unfortunate fight with Mary-Anna, and the reoccurring flashbacks. Sky only saw another human when they took her food and drink, and her only routine walks allowed were for the use of the bathroom. There was no sign of Lucy at all. Feeling lonely with only her subconscious for communication as per usual, she was suffering inside and she knew that no one could fully comprehend, nor, she felt, cared.

Knowing her next victim needed dealing with once the DNA results came in from the other two murders, she had to find out what was going on out there in the real world before her demons in white coats worked out her actions. The next victim was now lined up and ready; it was just down to timing. This is what kept Sky going, knowing the completion was near, everything she had done was soon to be rewarded from within. The spell-chanting evil had nearly reached its victory stage and Sky then knew it was time to leave this hell and open her gates to her paradise. As her spell told her, darkly whispered, *'One's dream means one's secret. One's pain will be delivered. You will be unseen. One will become something while they become nothing. To end one's secret will mean to end you. To end you means you have succeeded'.*

Sky knew that only time was on her side and not those in long white coats, her demons or Lucy Jenkins. Sky was determined to convince Lucy into believing her mind state and not just fobbing her off like the other cases she had come across. Sky wanted recognition for her powers and the way she has mastered something that life did not produce. Sky did not want to pass through her hell without sharing her knowledge with someone when the time was right. The exact person to share it with was Lucy. Sky wanted to covert her small-minded aptitude to take on board the way a creation can affect a so-called mental patient. Sky did not want to die a fruit loop. She wanted to die and be known as a destroyer. She needed Lucy's attention; she could not leave her hell without showing them what they were searching for...what were they in fact looking for? A murderer, a sicko, a mental patient, they did not even know themselves?

Sky had learned her lesson for life: hate, and everything is hated. Now she had sold her soul to the evil that creeps around thin air and delivers the crime that devolved from a special girl. Years' worth of stings from a group of blood-sucking pricks. Sky cared for nothing; nothing could make up for her anguish, nor could anyone help her. She wanted out and she wanted to take them all out with her. The more her mind wrapped around her past and the normal scum that had taken a piece of her will to live, the more she hated them for it.

Sky paced up and down in her throttled room, up and down again and again. Her head nodded fast in circular movements while her fingers played piano movements at her sides. She knew in the back of her mind that she had nowhere to run to, or nowhere to hide. With no one who cared, or even knew where she had gone. She did not even have a home, and she never chose to fall into this trap life made for her. Sky blamed every single one of them, wanting to tell each and every single one of them to just fuck off and die, with which she could, with free speech and all, but then there's always some sucker who wants to sue.

Why did society have the right to lock her up, its people in the obliteration league, those that rule the world, those that terrorise the world and the people in it, they needed locking up in those bloody straightjackets, to protect humanity from extinction? Definetly not, special people like Sky.

They had their priorities all wrong. Big boys and their toys; go on, keep pricking us. We are all born with some form of madness inside of us in some way or another. The world that only turns counter clockwise while backwards is all we know, around and around we all go. When the future looks rosy and the world moves on, we get bombed or threatened with the Euro. Not forgetting shootings, perverts, and everything sick, round and around we go.

They are the ones who needed locking up. Is it really worth it?

Therefore, for Sky's mother to have her born and develop into a world of nastiness with no protection, this Sky could never forgive. No one asked her mother to give birth to an oddball, so why this was allowed? Sky could never figure out. Shouldn't people have a surveyor or something come around and check before unprotected sex is granted? Wouldn't this make things better for unloved children dragged into a world of total despair, shouldn't we be asked first? Alternatively, why can't we pick our own parents? All those poor babies and youngsters dying from abuse, it makes you wonder why the surveyor gave permission. So-called human rights, our god, our surveyor, and our reckless decisions. Ever heard of condoms?

Everyone is full of hate, everyone has an enemy, and we all have one of those red buttons waiting to be hit. It is a shame that when the doctor dangles us at birth by our foot that a two-way ticket does not fall from the mother's love canal, with an option in later years to go back from where we came...our father's ball bags.

Sky could only sum up the judgments that rocked her mind by blaming the faults of others. Thus, the best thing for her to do was to let go of all that denial and face fact. We're better off dead...Sky's feelings exactly.

So the question is this, is Lucy the doctor facing a mental person born with hate or is it a person who has seen nothing but hate? On the other hand, Lucy who is mad and Sky who is normal? Why does the one in the straightjacket automatically have this label pinned to them?

Maybe it's because we, society, don't like free spirits. As Sky would say, think before you answer the question. Are you unhappy from people's nasty pricks and do you hate? If you tick yes in the questionnaire, then you are halfway there, halfway to madness. Sky ticked yes and now she's classified mental. Ask yourself, are you like her?

Come out of the closet and join them, don't worry about the huge label that's going to sit on your forehead. It doesn't matter, once you take this step your life will never be the same again. What is more, it will really hurt. So ask yourself the question, are you a Sky?

Is Sky mad? Who actually decides if you or I are mad? Who made the rule? How do we not know that the people who made the rule were not already mad themselves? There is nothing wrong with free spirits that walk our world.

PAIN FOR THE SANE

'You know the feeling when you're sitting there, alone, and the hurt rushes around your heart area, freezing from the cold heart that hides from within. The aching so severe while thinking of a way out, but you know you just cannot do it. Not because you are scared, nowhere near it, but because you have something to prove, something to show, waiting for someone to tell you "No, don't do it, I love you". Well, I'm still waiting for that person to say this to me, but no one did. I doubt that anyone ever will.

'Tears would form in my eyes. One by one they would plunge, my continued snivelling nearly choking me, but when I turn around for help no one is there. I doubt they ever will be. No one was ever there. I would just sit lonely for hours, I would look at one spot in front of me and I would just be staring hard; my blinking stopped for ages while the teardrops represented my life. The light would make my tears reflect my misery when I looked on. My storm of joint puffing smoke would drift out from my mouth slowly but smoothly whirling about the air I hated to breathe back in. The smoke would drift away from me and I could see my heaven like an animated cloud waiting for me, calling for me.

'The feeling of isolation is so demeaning but one feeling I'm now used to. I hated the truth and this truth was fact…the fact was, no one wanted me ever from day one. I had to live these seventeen years knowing this fucking fact. This is not because I was a nasty child, far from it. I do not know why it is; fact is right now in my life I could not care less for why it was. I do not have one caring bone in my body. I certainly have no regrets, regrets for killing normal scum that is'.

Lucy sat silently while hearing Sky's gloomy, sad words gush her way.

'I mean, what am I supposed to do? What is there for me to do? It's far too late now, I can't go back, but you know what, I don't want to go back', Sky said.

'It's never too late, Sky, to help yourself. You know this, surely if you help me to help you we could help each other'. Lucy smiled persuasively.

'Do not patronise me please. Remember the high IQ level. Yes, that's right, quit while you're ahead, Lucy. This is my game, do not try to take over, I'm in control and I will tell you my shit when I'm good and ready'.

Sky put her head down, a position she often used when feeling isolated and held it up with her hands, elbows on the white table.

'Sky, as I told you at the start of this meeting, at first I believed you made this whole story up because you're ill. Now I think differently. We know Jimmy killed Mrs Turner. We also now know since today that Tina killed Jimmy and Tina's results will be faxed to me in the next couple of days. However, we both know there is more to this story, don't we'? Lucy started to rub on her neck and twist it, trying to wake it up. The pair had been sitting there for almost two hours.

'I know already who killed whom. I planned the who-killed-whom procedure, for crying out loud', Sky croaked.

'Why don't you tell me all about this spell stuff. I think that would be the best place to start, don't you'? Lucy lifted the paper cup and sipped at her tea, waiting for her to begin. Sky persisted on.

'I got home, must have been around 4.30, it takes me awhile to get home. I like to drag it out. I had nothing to rush back to, you see. My auntie was never home anyway. I walked alone, I always did, even when certain kids lived near me and were walking the same way as me but chose never to walk alongside me. They would walk right past me. I guess I amused them on that particular day with sticky white gum in my hair, from fucking stupid bitch Tina. I hope she burns in hell.

'Well, when I got in after the confrontation with Mrs Turner I tried so bloody hard to get the gum out of my hair, but I couldn't. I then reached for a half joint while looking for cutters. It did not calm me one bit. I found the cutters then jumped to my bed. Next to me was a black box with a gold dove on top, my secret stash. I threw back two pills and swallowed a few mouthfuls of sherry; I turned on my Nirvana CD and blared it. Then I heard the words "nature's a whore" and then it fucking hit me'.

'What hit you, Sky'? Lucy asked.

'That Tina was a fucking whore, that everyone in this world is out to hurt others. That the world is such a dark place. Everyone screws everyone in one way or another, natural whores, as I said'. Lucy looked on at Sky puzzled, but she secretly understood her view on that subject.

'You have been screwed, haven't you, Lucy? I can see it in your eyes, come on tell me, I can see it. Someone stabbed you in the back, am I right'? Sky insisted.

'Yes, I have been hurt before, but hasn't everyone'?

'Tell me what happened'.

'Sky, we are here to chat about you and the murders, not about me'.

'Tell me, or I say nothing else to you'.

'Okay, I was cheated on a year ago, now that's it, okay? It's now past and I have learnt my lesson in life just like you are, Sky', Lucy uncomfortably replied.

'Seeeeee, as I said filthy whores, that is exactly what Adam did to me. Him and Tina, Tina of all people, how could he do that to me? He said he loved me for crying out loud. I let it go, but inside it killed me. I carried on seeing him, but each day that came, I hated him more, and that is also why she is dead, the bitch. Never trust a male, never, they are animals. They have this urge to cheat, they have built-in animal characteristics. They are so goddamn weak'.

'Who is Adam'? Lucy quizzed.

'I don't want to chat about him, I'm telling you about what annoys me, okay'?

Lucy really wanted to know about this Adam, who he was, if he was involved in the murders, if he was dead too. Lucy would wait for the right moment to bring it back up and find out just who this Adam really was. 'Okay, fine'.

'And do you want to know what else really annoys me? Everyone is always misjudging other people's words. They hear what is said but don't translate its meaning. I really hate that. There are always two sides to a story, two sides to a word and to a meaning and not just the clear obvious one that springs to mind'. Sky looked up in Lucy's direction.

'Sky, you are baffling here? I'm not understanding you now'.

'Shut the fuck up and listen then. What I mean without a doubt is this, when someone says absolutely nothing, they are clearly saying a hell of a lot, and when someone is saying a hell of a lot, they are clearly meaning nothing at all. Second-hand gossip is looked upon as truth, while truth is looked upon as total madness. Now, Miss Jenkins, you and your cronies have me here under madness so I guess I'm chatting the absolute truth. So, explain that to me please. Whores, the whole lot of you', Sky scowled, her nearly healed face looking tired.

'Sky, I'm trying to believe, but it's quite hard to believe that firstly someone could make such evil, and secondly it really happening with no explanation. Keep explaining the spell because I do not get it, you keep jumping from one thing to the other. The spell, tell me about the spell'. Lucy started to bite away at her bottom lip in annoyance.

'Look, I will say it in simple words to you. I made a spell in my room, I will tell you exactly what happened. As the CD turned I was collecting items for my practice; I had my dagger, my chalice, my blood and my drugs. By now I was on my fifth pill. I don't usually take that many, mind you, but anyway I was drinking and smoking and I will admit that I got a bit carried away. In all honesty, I think I was totally wrecked, out of my skull. I was under candlelight by now, with a strand of sticky white-gummed hair in one hand and the dagger in the other. The colours were wild and the fabrications of 3-D images were running around madly before me. I burnt the sticky white-gummed hair in the chalice, mixed with my blood after cutting a fine line across my heart area, to signify my pain, and fuck that hurt I tell you.

'I burnt under the tin, frying it away over a candle. It boiled and stunk. I chanted a spell, my own spell, and next thing I knew was that I awoke in the morning in a ball on the other side of the room, naked. There was no sign of anything I had used that night and everything was back in its original place. I looked in the mirror and my hair was back to its normal length plus the colour had changed to blonde, but how? I fucking cut it off, the sticky gum, didn't I? I certainly never dyed my hair because I don't do dyes.

'And that's when things did become very confusing. I had to explain it all to myself. I could only remember selected bits at first, but it's when I dreamt about Mrs Turner, or you could call it her nightmare, that's when things came clear. The next day, as the news played, everything came flooding back to me. The rest is now history, except for what I have planned for the very near future'.

* * *

As those words left Sky's mouth, her smile grew.

'What are your plans. Sky, what do you have planned'? Lucy was really trying to trip Sky up, trying to make her slip up on her many concealed words.

'Wouldn't you like to know? But I wouldn't want to spoil things, you have to earn the answers to your questions'.

'Don't you care, don't you care about what you are saying you have done or going to do'? Lucy demanded.

'What is there to care for, I mean, does anybody care about anyone but themselves'?

'Yes, I care for others, I bet you do too, deep down inside, but I think you're afraid to admit this to yourself, Sky'.

Sky stood quickly and threw a chair, a mad white-coloured chair, to the other side of the room. She started dancing in a ritual manner fast and furious pushing her hands outwards and moving her fingers about the silent air while her top arms were swaying from side to side, like a moving snake on the sands. Sky started screaming. 'Join me, join meeeeeeee, Lucy'. Jumping up and down and around fast then slowly up then down, she laughed.

'Sky, what are you doing? Sit down, will you now'? Lucy shouted to her in shock.

'I'm dancing in your funny farm, Lucy, join me, join me, Lucy'. Sky jumped onto the white table and continued her antics in front of Lucy's face.

'Sit down right now. If you do not then I will have no choice but to call for security'. Lucy stood with her hands placed on the table, leaning forward.

'Lucy, join me, believe me, do not be against me, I'm not mad, I have a wonderful killing tool to cleanse my hate. Do not make me hate you too. Say you believe me then I will help you close this case'. Sky constantly danced freely on the table pushing her hands out to grab at Lucy's hands, to pull her on to the table to join her.

'Tell me about Adam, I want to know about him'! Lucy shouted, still leaning forward over the table.

'Join me up here, dance with me, feel it, think it, then I will show you it'. Lucy took Sky's hands and joined her to the top of the white table.

'Tell me, Sky, tell me who killed Tina'.

'Dance, just feel it. Close your eyes and hear my words'. Lucy gave in and slowly copied Sky's strange dance as she half closed her eyes.

'Adam is alive but will soon meet his death; and you will be there to see and you will be there to feel. I will guide you to his death. I will show you how but I will not tell you when, you will feel when. I won't tell you where, you will feel where but you will be too late to help. Adam killed Tina. Yet he does not even know this fact. Tina killed Jimmy, but did not know this fact. Jimmy killed Mrs Turner, but did not know this fact'. Sky wickedly laughed.

'How, Sky, how'? Lucy shouted again, peeping from beneath her half-closed eyes.

'From my head, Lucy, from within me, I set them up, I made them kill each other but they did not, if you get me. It was all meeee'. Sky started jumping uncontrollably.

'So what you're saying is that you dreamt it and then it happened, but no one was there, just this evil, you call it. You left their DNA or some kind of proof so it would point to them and not you, is that what you're saying, Sky? Just say it, will you'! Lucy shouted harder for an overdue answer.

'You're so fucking quick it makes me sick. Yes, Lucy, I did it all. I set them up, they were whores, all of them, I'm the special one. I am the evil'.

'Crap! What a load of crap! I don't believe it, there's no way', Lucy stated. Sky jumped off the white table to the floor and slowly turned to face Lucy once again. Sweat dripped from her hairline and rolled into little balls, her eyes glowing with truth, she looked like the evil. She raised her arms into the air in a star shape position, her head rolling around on top of her shoulders. She stopped. Lucy had stopped; she stood still looking like a scared girl put on show looking silly on top of a white table.

'I dreamt them doing the act in my head, Lucy, then while I dream the evil leaves me and carries it out. What it sees in my head and the people who are there, then the evil represents them, the evil turns into them, hence the DNA'.

'No way, I don't believe that', Lucy said, shaking her head with scepticism.

'He will be hung, Lucy, where we first made love. I will relieve him of his deceit and total betrayal. I have left the best until last. I will guide you, I will teach you. You will never meet another fruit loop like me again, so make sure you take those notes of yours, you're going to be shocked', Sky sniggered dangerously.

'Say...Lucy, let me ask you. You read Tina's case file. Did you like the way I controlled Tina's death? Did you like the way I used her own underwear to tie her up? Her fishnet tights bound her arms and ankles, and her black g-string, the pair I guessed she could have wore when she FUCKED my boyfriend, stuffed inside her big gob.

'Lucy, would you like to know the reason I sat upon her wobbly fence that night she was killed? I sat there to feel her raped. Penetrations jolted the fence and shivered up my spine. I needed to see and feel under her window that inside that room Tina was being raped and killed. The black shadows jumping around her room, I guess that is when she sustained her huge injuries from my dark evil. What a rush!

'Now you all sit and wait for the proof, from whom the fuck ever you get your proof from. You know that I left proof for you all, like I did with them all. For crying out loud, how easy can this be?

'The poor girl had no hope in the world of being saved, and Adam was doing his thing elsewhere and little miss pick on me please sat and watched outside her window in the tree. So, fuck you and fuck her…fuck you all'.

Lucy shook her head in disbelief as she turned away from a cock-and-bull story and then left the room, slamming the door behind her.

'That's it, quick, Lucy, run, run, go find out who this Adam is. Don't let me slow you down. Run, rabbit, run. Although you're too late, way too late', Sky said.

BEST FOR LAST

The white clock that hung behind the reception desk, behind the large lady that sat on night watch, struck midnight. The large lady read a women's magazine and ate away at hospital sandwiches, half asleep. The ward floor whispered a silence; the lights dimmed except the single spotlight which hit the large lady, hiding the white clock that hung behind the reception desk, which now struck five past midnight.

All the mental people for that ward were asleep from an exciting day of therapy meetings, exhausting walks pacing up and down and to and from all facing walls. The smell of sweat came from the overcrowded patients, with a touch of over-urinated, blue-striped bedcovers coming from the ones with the weak bladders, or from being too lazy to ring the bell for the pot pan, which they hated so much to use.

Hidden away at the end of the ward in a padded cell still, reclined a sleeping Sky. She knew what she had to do while she slept, she had saved the best until last and she had to deal with it. As she slept, she was in deep preparation for her next murder. As she lay, her image blurred, her hair was turning to a light blonde shade, magically altering. She looked somewhat enhanced; she looked much more slender around her cheekbones and eye sockets, her face looked tighter than normal, and in her hand, she held something so powerful, her creation, her phenomenon. Something that only showed itself and worked in the conduct of evil. Something that only Sky could control.

* * *

On the other side of the ward, Lucy sat in her office reading all the interviews that held Sky's confessions of the murders. She repeatedly went over them trying so hard to find some truth, something and anything that would make sense, something to work on to help close the case. She just could not fully believe what Sky had told her, she did not know what to believe and at this hour, she could not believe anything. Lucy needed sleep desperately, but fought it back and continued to read and write her conclusions that she had now memorized. She waited for a phone call for an update on this Adam. The police were searching details of all Adams that lived in Sky's area, and the victim's areas, within a ten-mile surrounding distance. In the morning, they would search the schools and hospitals, and in their own databases. They would question the victim's families and friends; they would get back to Lucy ASAP. Lucy's hand took the gold-framed picture that stood on her desk; she smiled at the picture of herself and her child, Cindy. After staring, she returned it to its place and carried on.

* * *

The large lady by now had finished all four of her hospital sandwiches and started washing her leftover solids about her mouth with diet coke. Why ever she drank diet coke was anyone's guess, as she pulled open the top drawer of the desk and heaved a brown paper bag full of wine gums and out dropped a candy bar. A good guess is that she drank the diet coke to feel like she was contributing somewhat to her low-fat diet in some small way.

The large lady ripped desperately at her sealed chocolate and hand slammed it into her saliva-saturated mouth and she gnarled at it with a pleasing smile. Her cheekspuffed out like a hamster's. As she finished her last bite, she rolled the wrapper into a tight ball and placed it precisely onto the desk while her tongue stretched out for the last remaining nuts to chew. Suddenly, she heard a huge bang. The bang came from Lucy's office.

The large lady jerked forward and pushed back at her chair as she headed fast down the grey disinfected stone-floored corridor towards Lucy's office and knocked at her door.

'Mrs Jenkins, are you okay in there'? the large lady enquired. There was no reply, the large lady grabbed at the door handle and pushed down onto it. As she did this, the door refused to open up, as if a force stood on the inside and refused her to enter without permission. She pushed harder but still the door would not budge. The large lady stood back, she breathed and then she threw her weight and pulled down hard. She then fell head first into the office.

To her astonishment, she saw Lucy up against the wall, moving along slowly, her feet an inch off the ground. The large lady puffed into the palms of her hands with her eyes nearly popping from their sockets, in disbelief she couldn't move, to speak or to even help the rising Lucy. Lucy's eyes closed shut, just peacefully rising slowly up the wall. The large lady watched, but did nothing.

'Mrs Jenkins, what on earth are you doing'? the large lady screamed.

The large lady ran to Lucy's body after convincing herself she was not seeing things nor going mad, it was actually happing before her eyes. As she hung onto her ankles above her black high-heeled shoes to stop her from rising higher, fret pouring from the large lady's body as she struggled to pull her back down. Lucy started mumbling and it got louder as she swayed slightly, then more violently from side to side across the wall.

"One's dream, one's secret. One's pain will be delivered. You will be unseen. One will become something while they become nothing. To end one's secret will mean to end you. To end you means you have succeeded'.

Lucy constantly mumbled the words with a voice that now was not her own, a voice of the devil, deep and clear full of hate. A voice, a familiar one that sounded like Sky's, but now deeper, hoarse, scary but seductive, Sky's voice mixed with darkness. As her head hit the top of the ceiling with a hard bang, blood started to show through her white blouse, around her heart area, like leaking ink on a piece of blotting paper, soaking up the fresh loose fluid. Like Sky's mother too, when she was shot down by the East boy, like Tina with a slit across her heart area when she was found dead. Sky, when she first started her evil, had slit across her own heart area to signify her pain when she chanted and encouraged her evil to come, the evil pleasing Sky's requests by leaving a trademark of revulsion on everyone else's body...her sufferers.

The large lady took one look, her eyes rolled to the back of her head, eyelashes fluttering, shaking as she fainted with a loud thud. Lucy's floating body slid back down the wall with blood trail lines, like a slimy snail on its mission to spurn laid-down salts, and she slowly stood in a zombie-like stance. Her eyes hit the large lady crashed on the floor. She then looked about her office, and something polished caught her eye.

She grabbed at the silvery object that sat on her desk and then walked over to the body that lay on her floor. Her hands held tight around the silver sharp, pointed object and she plunged sadistically into the large lady's stomach, blood pissing out like a pierced king-size waterbed. She dropped the sharp silver letter opener to the floor, after sticking into the large lady's stomach a few times more. Heading out of her office, she knocked her right knee on the edge of her desk and nearly fell, but Lucy did not once turn back around to look at the scandal she left behind.

Sky was still asleep, but her appearance returned to its normal state. She slept like a baby as her body curled into a ball and one hand pulled the covers completely over her head. Something she had started was soon to end.

WHO KILLED WHOM?

The sun set and early birds flew as Lucy cried into her bloodstained hands. She remembered Nicky, the large lady and her dead body. She had killed her. She was a cold-blooded murderer, and she knew this. Was she to go on the run or hand herself in? Were the police looking for her as she sat deeply in the woodlands? She was too confused. Her brain wrapped around the many words she asked herself. She did not have one nasty bone in her body, and she could never kill a fly, never mind another human.

She remembered sticking the silver sharp letter opener into the large lady's body, but zilch before. What could have possibly made her do such an act? she kept asking.

Lucy stood to her feet and looked around the quiet, bluebell flourished woodland she was in the middle of, but she did not recognise where she stood. She had never wandered into these woods before, and she was misplaced.

She slowly headed off pushing back some loose branches, her white shirt ripped and covered in blood still, her hair looking chaotic. She felt tired, angry, and shocked. She cried with no energy.

'Hello, is anybody out there? Can someone help me? I'm lost, please, someone...anyone'.

Lucy continued to walk in an uneven line, trying to find some kind of path or opening to a road from the woods. Panting hard and tripping from uproot stumps, she heard a whistle coming from in front of her and shouted, 'Hello! Can you hear me? I need some help! I am lost'! No reply came back. She started running north in the direction the whistling came from. As she ran the noise became louder, and she looked around but saw nothing.

Slowing right down near to a halt, she saw a movement out of the corner of her eye. She saw a figure in denim jeans, black top and blonde dreadlocks under his black cap, walking mindlessly in the opposite direction to her, whistling. He was carrying something. Lucy was too scared to call to him (stuck in the woods, a man and a woman alone...anything could happen) so she silently followed behind him about a hundred feet out of sight, hoping he would lead her to a safe road. As she stared, she saw him slowly chuck his denim jacket onto the ground. He carried on, as if it was planned. She hurried when he was almost out of sight to the jacket to see if it carried anything of help, like a mobile.

Her hand hunted every pocket but nothing, until she felt a leather wallet hidden away deeply and pulled it out. Going through the contents, she pulled out his driving license and looked at the name that sent trembles down her aching spine. A Mr Adam Hunt. She continued and pulled out a picture, a picture of Sky with this mystery Adam, whom Sky so hated. Behind the picture was a piece of lined paper with the words in big capitals.

Lucy fell back and choked. She could not stop choking, and nearly puking from crying so hard, she looked again at the note.

DEAR LUCY

NO ONE KNOWS THAT YOU KILLED HER, ALL IS SAFE. COME TO SEE ME BEFORE THE END COMES TO ME FIRST. I DID TRY OTHER WAYS TO CONVINCE YOUR MIND BUT YOU DISMISSED ALL, SO THEREFORE I HAD TO TURN TO DRASCTIC MEASURES. YOU LEARNED THE HARD WAY!

LOVE, SKY

Lucy looked up and wiped away the slobber from her mouth, realising Adam had now gone from view, and dropping the contents, she ran after him.

* * *

Adam had stopped next to a homemade camp with a chequered blanket hanging from a branch, clammy now and still torn from when Sky placed it onto the ground for their first night of passion. He now faced his dues from his deceit and total betrayal.

He took one end of the long piece of thick towrope, which he carried with him, and tied it around his neck and then pulled out a double-edged dagger from his wallet, hidden in his big desert army boot. He threw the rest of the rope over his shoulder. He started to climb the tree that the camp sat around.

Going only halfway up, he tied the other end of the towrope around the single branch that came off the main tree. 'Sky, I loved you', he bellowed into the air. 'I'm sorry'.

Lucy hid behind the gathered trees now; she did not want to lose sight of the man that could hold all clues to the murders. She watched on, not realising fully what he was doing at first, as she looked up into the tree and saw his nude fit body. Lucy was shocked and somewhat shy by what she saw, as he chucked his belongings directly below him.

He forced the double-edged dagger into his sorry heart, and then pulling it back out crying in pain, he did it again. 'Noooooo'! Lucy finally shouted in a delayed reaction from fright and numbness.

In slow motion, his feet shifted to the edge of the branch and into the air, and as he jumped, he tasted his last breath for life; he tasted Sky's evil. He was under her power from start to finish; all he had to do was love her the way she needed loving. As he fell he felt her power, he hung himself.

A snap of bone confirmed his death and the result of his betrayal showed from his rocking stiff cadaver. There he would wait for his mistress to join him, the evil gates to Sky's heaven he will wander and await. The list of hated, their souls dismembered and unable to be free, Sky was successful.

Lucy screamed hard and lost her steadiness, falling backward. She rolled down the wooden slant banging into trees, still declining. She landed onto a small stoned road, where she lay a broken woman.

* * *

Back at the hospital where Lucy worked and Sky slept the police and ambulance services swarmed the building. News reporters and the public stood waiting for updates, pushed back by forensics police who probed the perimeter.

Sky was awake pacing her padded cell as she always did. She could not stop smiling to herself, and something or someone amused her. Jumping onto her solid bed, laughing at the young man in a long white coat that came for routine injections as his assistant took Sky's breakfast tray away. He could not control her as she taunted at him.

'One's dream, one's secret. One's pain will be delivered. You will be unseen. One will become something while they become nothing. To end one's secret will mean to end you. To end you means you have succeeded', Sky sang, still jumping and pointing out her first finger to the young man in the white coat.

The young man left the room to get additional help. He was too afraid of her, he couldn't handle her on his own. 'You fucking whores! Adam, die! Die, you bastard'! she screamed, a joyous scream. Then the door reopened and this time, four long white coats came her way. Sky knew what was to come next and ran around in circles, like a crazed dog chasing his tail.

'Come get me, you mudderfuckers'! Sky shouted as she body-slammed one of the white coats to the floor and started to strangle at her neck, holding tight, squeezing hard.

The other three white coats jumped onto Sky and injected her once again, the prick she so detested. Sky was thrown to her bed and strapped back on with the white straightjacket in place; she spat at one of the white coats.

'I have won! I have conquered, and I will see you all in hell'!

THE WHOLE TRUTH AND NOTHING BUT THE TRUTH

Lucy Jenkins' head gradually rolled around her shoulders then to the back of her neck. She had finally made it back home after walking three miles from the road she fell onto and hitchhiking to her local town. Hot water sprinkled down her nude, bruised goose-bumped body, removing traces of blood and dirt, but the water was unable to remove any trace of guilt. Her murdering hands cupped over her head, helping the water over her dyed red hair, now straight from the water stretching out each loose curl. This broken woman needed answers to her questions and there was only one person available that could answer them.

Lucy turned the gold-effect two-way bath and shower mixer taps off and the other hand grabbed out for the scarlet coloured bath towel. Wrapping her body with the towel, she stepped out from her bathroom into her bedroom, having to be quick before Mrs Smith returned with little Cindy. It was almost 3 p.m. Pushing her right foot into the opening of her black cropped trousers then pulling them up, she jumped on to her bed. Her black laced bra strap slipped down her shoulder and she pulled it back up as she leaned for the phone.

'Hello, it's Lucy Jenkins here, can you tell me if anyone has phoned for me or if anyone is looking for me at my office, Sara'?

'Really…no one at all. What? Last night…erm, I left early. What time did that happen then? Are the police still there?

* * *

'Murdered! Oh my god! Well, I am on my way down, say half an hour…okay, then, Sara, see you then'.

Lucy fell back onto her bed after the phone call and nervously bit away at her bottom lip. Thinking to herself about the phone call she just had, going back over the tone and the words, was Sara's voice genuine? Sara did not sound different. Sara and Lucy's relationship was friendly and Sara would have warned Miss Jenkins if something were erroneous in the mental institution. Lucy finished dressing and collected her belongings after leaving a note for Cindy and Mrs Smith, saying she was to be late that night and to have sweet dreams, love from Mum. She then headed to the place that held a Miss Sky Shanti.

* * *

The air was stuffy but the zephyr warm as the children left for home. Hundreds of feet thumped the ground as they ran away from their classrooms, jumping into their parents' safe arms, while some children cycled home or jumped into the family car.

Home time, the best time for most, but for Sky as a youngster this was her worst time. No one ever picked her up, no one ever walked her home, and for her there was neither a bike nor car, only her sweeping forlorn feet pacing the hot gravel.

Mrs Smith held her elderly hands out to catch Cindy's young, petite hands as she led her out from the school entrance.

'You have yourself a nice day there, little Cindy'? A soft affectionate voice came from Mrs Smith.

'Yes, I did Mommy a picture today and I did sand today with Sam and he flicked it in my hair, so I left him on his own cos I didn't want to tell him off but I didn't want sand in my hair. Ooh, I also ate all my dinner and I played outside longer today and we had the bikes out. It was fun'. Cindy skipped, swaying their arms back and forth.

'You sure did have yourself a nice day, and for being well it looks like you have yourself chocolate ice cream on the menu for when we get back'. Mrs Smith laughed.

* * *

Back at the hospital, Lucy walked apprehensively and slowly away from the lift doors and followed the disinfected grey stoned corridor floor to her office, which was now taped up with thick yellow police tape. There were only a few bodies rushing around now, as the dead body had already been removed and the investigation team had been in and out. Lucy could not enter the room, no one was allowed to enter, not that she felt she could or needed to. She stood side by side with the doorframe opening and slowly she twisted around her bruised body and now looked deep into her office. The memories soon flooded back, she couldn't look for more than five seconds and then she found herself scampering furiously back the other way.

'Sara'! Lucy shouted.

'Yes, Miss Jenkins, what can I do for you, are you okay'?

'Sara, yes I'm okay. If anybody wants me, I will be in a meeting with Sky. I have a few more questions to ask her'.

'But Miss Jenkins, you are scheduled to see Mr Sanderson in half an hour with Mary-Anna. What should I say'? Sara rudely interrupted.

'Cancel it and arrange another appointment, please'. Lucy walked off. Sara watched her walk back past the reception desk and into the ward.

Lucy looked about the ward. The in-patients were doing their twice-weekly industrial therapy, over twenty patients. It only lasted two hours, which was long enough before anyone got bored. Woodwork, painting, sewing and all things you do with your hands. Supervision for each activity, the noises of the hammer banging while the paint dripped, just like in a nursery, like the kids getting excited with the sounds of stimulation.

Lucy walked over to the head nurse and whispered into her ear. For a while they both whispered to each other. Lucy then turned around, she took a deep breath, and she left that ward. The head nurse headed to Mary-Anna to tell her that the meeting she was waiting for with Mr Sanderson and Miss Jenkins was cancelled. With that, Mary-Anna walked off in a paroxysm to the corner of the room.

Lucy stood outside the door that led into the room that held Sky. She felt nervous and wary, like everything that had happened to her in the last 24 hours was an authentic, tailored nightmare but she hoped it was just a sinister dream, a confusing tiring dream. However, she knew she had killed her...did she kill her? She kept debating. But what if she was wrong, was she to bring it up and confess or to just simply forget it all and wait until someone questioned her. Why had she not already been questioned? she thought. What about the cameras all around the building, what about if someone had seen her leave? What if this and what if that. Her mind skipped around the words. Lucy walked in only fifty minutes after Sky's second pinpricked injection... the doctors had used Modicate.

The doctors tried to find the right dose and drug. They believed one of them was able to calm and help her. Her prick holes by now were doubling up on each of her inner arms. No drug so far seemed to help, and she was getting worse. They had doubled the dose now. Each dose she was given sailed her bloodstream and performed no action of relevance. However, the last dose seemed to have affected her somewhat.

THE END IS NIGH

Sky sat on the floor with her back facing the door. Lucy tip-toed only a few inches away from the white painted wall that looked yellowy as she entered and shut the door behind her. She walked around slowly, feeling like she had just been caught stealing or doing something she shouldn't have been doing, when the words spoke aloud.

'Well, well, look who it ain't, good timing', Sky said still facing her back to the door. 'You took your time, for a while I didn't think you would come, but then I knew you would have to, as you urgently require the answers to your questions, don't you'?

With that, Sky turned and lifted her head at a snail's pace; the pair caught each other's eyes, the feeling immense, dark and scary. The way Sky looked intimidated Lucy, but Lucy also felt captivated and somehow liberated. Lucy was ready for any kind of cock-and-bull story force fed to her now; she was ready to face the truth…Sky's truth.

Sky looked flushed as her pink dry tongue popped out from her mouth, lifting up her top lip, as she tried to share the moisture in her mouth, but her mouth was dry.

'Do not be shy,Lucy', she said. 'Would you like me to start? Would you like me to confirm to you whether you killed her or not. Yes. Okay, I will, it was you but you did it because of me, and with much gratitude, I thank you. I believe now that you have opened your mind and crossed the parallel lines before you. I am sorry to have put your mind through such lunacy, but with such little alternative I had no other way of making you heed my words without judging me, like the way your job title requests you to. As I said when we first met, and I will say it again, I am not mad…I am special'.

'Sky, cut the crap. Did I kill Nicky or not? That is all I want to know'.

'Yes'.

'So I am a murderer, but how, why would I? What is going on around here? Please enlighten me'.

'Shut up, Lucy, and I will'.

'No, no, let me guess. I guess this is where your story comes in. Let me presume you are going to tell me you dreamt it and it happened, and this time it was I you dreamt doing such sickness'.

'Yes, correct'. Sky's face dispensed sweat as she answered the questions that Lucy threw at her. 'And let me guess, you already know about Adam, don't you, Sky? Of course you do, I MEAN, HELLO, LUCY, WAKE UP! You dreamt that too, didn't you'? she said, raising her hands.

'Yes'.

'Now what bugs me is this, Sky. Okay, let's say I did kill her and the note I read in the woods was genuine. So if I'm safe, as you tell me, and it doesn't point to me being the murderer, then who does it point to? Who's taking the blame for this one, Sky'?

'Me'.

'You'?

'Yes'.

Lucy laughed loud and hard, while an insane smirk crossed her chops. This woman who killed, who watched a hanging, who faced a sad case, and who couldn't get her mind to focus, could not feel anything else but laughter shake her system.

'I should have guessed that one too; I mean how original can you get, Sky? So let me just run through this one more time. Please feel free to butt in at any time in case I get anything wrong. Jimmy murdered Mrs Turner, Tina murdered Jimmy, Adam murdered and raped Tina and Adam kills himself. Suicide, that's what you drove him to. You then set me up to kill Nicky the receptionist, just to prove a sick point to me. Now what happens, can you please tell me that'?

Sky clapped her hands as she stood and walked past Lucy, the walls speeding around and around. She took a deep breath, then stopped.

'You are correct, that is ten points to you. What happens next is up to you now'.

'What do you mean'?

'Well, this is where the fun starts for you. As you are my prescribed doctor, you are the one that has to give feedback to your mentor. You are the one who has to come to a decision whether I am mad or not. Now let's just run through the evidence we have. Can you actually verify that I killed any of them, even though you know that I did it, can you prove this? I think not. Why can't you is the question, just one of your many questions that I will gladly answer for you'. Sky smiled a one-sided beam as her left eye refused to stay open. Sky continued.

'Well, it turns out that they all killed each other, for whatever reasons yourself and your cronies choose to blame, nothing points to me, which means I will not get convicted for any of these murders. On the other hand, I clearly would get charged for the murder of what's her face, ermm, oh yeah! Nicky, poor girl. That is going to cause such an uproar for your family loving institution you all have here. Anyway, I will not be around to share those moments to come'. Sky scratched her neck under her left ear, where a red rash had slowly showed itself on the surface of her skin.

'And that is a real shame, as I would really love to see you try to persuade the others about this story. They will think you are a complete and utter fool, no one will believe you and can you afford to look so small, I think not. What on earth will you do, Lucy…please enlighten me.'

'What do you mean? Okay, Sky, you win. You are intelligent and have succeeded in your fucked up game'.

'Succeeded, I have succeeded'.

'Yes, that is what I said, succeeded'.

'I know, I heard you the bloody first time, it just reminded me of my spell and what is to come next, that's all'.

'More murders? You have done enough, Sky, you have done enough damage'.

'Yes, just one more, Lucy, don't worry, and I know in the back of your head you wonder, you wonder if it's going to be you. You are the last person I would hurt. I'm not ashamed to say this now but well…I really do like you, Lucy, you have helped me significantly'.

Sky drifted across the small room again, her home, then back to the corner of her bed. She was not holding her balance as she would in general, and she faintly fell to the edge of the bed and sat stiffly on its blue-striped cover trying to hold her focus.

'Sky, that's great, I'm sure. I'm flattered, but the thing is this, you seem to be forgetting one thing, what you have done? You are a cold blooded killer'.

'Get off your high horse, Lucy, so are you. What is done is done; you will be fine, I'm sure. You have gained knowledge from me, and I'm positive that with the next patient you take on in the future, you will listen more and understand before you judge, I'm optimistic that your mind has opened up now'. With that remark, Lucy's face dropped.

'Sky, you sound as if we are saying our goodbyes. If you think you have gotten away with this then think again because you haven't. I will prove that you are mad. You're not special, and I will prove that you were the sole killer here'.

'Great, I hope you do. And believe me, when you're done, you will look an even bigger fool than you do now'. Sky expressed amusement and with that, she started to lightly shake. The soles of her feet were off the ground while her toes were shaking vibrations that shook her ankles all the way to her knees. Her hands and wrist areas shook to the same beat.

'What's wrong with you'? Lucy asked.

'Oh, nothing much, I'm just preparing for my long journey'.

'You're doing it again, quit the game, it's over. Stop fooling, stop your crap. What do you mean, your journey'?

'Look, it's only over simply because I am in the middle of ending it. Let's just say goodbye and I will leave knowing you have been good to me, a little slow, but you did well'.

'That's it. I have had it with you, I'm going to call the nurses in here to check you over'

'Fine'. With that, Lucy angrily headed to the door and struggled to open it...nothing. Just like the way Nicky the receptionist tried...but nothing, the door was not going to open unless informed to. On the bed lay Sky. She shook harder than she was only five minutes ago, and vex poured from her frown and her slowing down body, while her hand held her chest area. Her breathing or lack of was soft and little. Her hair was magically altered, changed to a blonde shade while her facial area turned slender, just like the same way it did when she dreamed her evil. Lucy looked on in disbelief and tried to shout for help. She was petrified; the words refused to fall out as she pulls at the door.

'Lucy, give up, there is no case, move on, take this as a learning experience, case closed', a weakening Sky muttered.

Lucy ran to Sky and held her in her arms delicately as she watched the young girl fade away, fading away from her misery. Sky was reaching to the light, the bright light she had dreamed of entering, the light that showed her dead victims, now ready and awaiting as her slaves. She saw when she arrived only halfway through the bright light that her sorry life was nearly far away from her, she was nearly successful, only a little further to go and she would be there.

'What is going on, what have you done? You did this to yourself, didn't you? Sky, stop it, PLEASE STOP IT'. Lucy's words suddenly dragged Sky back from her light. She only had to travel just that little bit further to get to her new home and now that familiar voice, Lucy's voice, was to blame for dawdling Sky's modus operandi. Sky replied.

'It is Morphine from my injection earlier. My overdose. I dreamt this moment. This is my planned death'. Sky found it too hard to release anymore verbal skills. The one thing she had learned in life was to express, but now silence had shunned her resonance.

' ...bye', Sky said, with her last struggle. She managed to fight the silence that shone before her. She could see the bright light once more.

Her breathing, still diminutive, faded by the second, and her heart rate dropped by the second. She held harder to her chest area as she drifted away from the cold bleak room. Her lonely heartbeat quivered as an alternative to a beating while Lucy held her tighter. A tear fell, she tugged at Sky's body, not knowing what was happening. The door facing her was refusing to let her out to get any help. What could she do?

Sky's existence fell into cardiac arrest. Lucy jumped up, placed Sky's body back onto the bed, and darted to the door that snubbs exit and pounds.

Within minutes, Sky's body rejects oxygen flow to her messed-up brain, to her thinking tool, to her dangerous mind games. To a place where she stored all memories, all actions and all words, everything in her short-lived life that she had captivated. Now it had disappeared, no trace of any memory. Surely now she could be happy. Sky was entirely in the light now. She walks through the gates of paradise.

'HELPPPP! Someone help me in here'. Still pounding...but nothing. Lucy looked back at Sky and saw that she needed help; Lucy knew she needed a defibrillator to shoot an electric shock, to retune her lonely heartbeat to the only thing needed to bring her back. As she looked harder, she saw Sky's last shake, her last breath, and her last word had already been said. While her last action had just that minute been delivered, Sky lying dead before her.

Lucy walked slowly to Sky's bedside and knelt to the floor, weeping. Lucy lifted her trembling hand above Sky's tranquil looking green glass eyes and closed them. She moved a strand of blonde shaded hair from her face that was stuck to her rosy cheek by sweat or even by a dropped tear. Lucy looked long and hard, then stood back to whisper, 'I like you too, Sky, I'm sorry'. Sorry for what, Lucy did not know, she just felt sorry for the dead girl she called Sky. Walking backwards, she then stopped with difficulty after seeing Sky's arm fall over the bedside. Something dropped out from Sky's unbending hand onto the floor. Lucy bent and picked it up, and to her surprise, as she looked down at the object, she shivered. It was a strand of burned black, white-gummed stale curly hair. The same white piece of sticky gummed hair Sky said she had burned in her chalice with her blood for her immoral spell. The same piece of sticky white gum Tina had stuck there in her hair all those months ago. Lucy held in her fingertips the cause to the deaths. How could she explain that to the others? How could she make out that her dead patient was mad when she knew deep down inside that her dead patient was, in fact, special...?

Printed in the United States
18605LVS00005B/406-441

9 781413 714258